LEGEND OF THE LOST

Dr. Lansdale's voice became lower as she recounted the story of the Borgia dagger. All of Tessa's guests leaned closer to hear.

"With the life flowing out of her, Marisol flung open the bedroom shutters, letting in the light of the full moon. And as she raised the dagger over Armando's bed, she screamed his name so loud they say it shattered the windows in the room."

By then Tessa's parlor had become so quiet, Frank could hear the beating of his own heart.

"From that day on, the legend goes, whoever takes possession of the dagger dies mysteriously within four months of having touched it."

Books in THE HARDY BOYS CASEFILES® Series

Available from ARCHWAY Paperbacks

THE HARDY BOYS CASEFILES NO. 13

THE BORGIA DAGGER

FRANKLIN W. DIXON

AN ARCHWAY PAPERBACK
Published by POCKET BOOKS
New York   London   Toronto   Sydney   Tokyo

AN ARCHWAY PAPERBACK *Original*

An Archway Paperback published by
POCKET BOOKS, a division of Simon & Schuster Inc.
1230 Avenue of the Americas, New York, N Y 10020

ISBN: 0-671-67956-2

First Archway Paperback Printing March 1988

10 9 8 7 6 5 4 3

Printed in the U.S.A.

IL 7+

Chapter

1

FRANK HARDY'S EYES widened. "Watch out!" he shouted. He ran to stop Callie Shaw before she took another step. With catlike reflexes, he sprang after her. Whipping his arm around her, he pulled her back just in time.

"Wh-what are you doing?" Callie sputtered as she stumbled backward over the dirt path and clutched Frank. She looked around for the unknown menace. But all she noticed was the swaying of the rushes in the wind, and the silver blue surface of the river as it raced by.

Frank loosened his grip. With a sigh of relief, he cast his glance down to a spot on the ground. "It's poison ivy," he said. "You just missed stepping in it."

Callie looked at him in disbelief. *"Poison ivy?"* she cried. "You scared me like that because of a little poison ivy? I thought we were in danger of losing our lives or something!"

"Well, poison ivy isn't a whole lot of fun, you know." Frank said, slightly embarrassed.

Callie straightened herself out and picked up the picnic basket she had dropped. "Frank, relax—you're not working today, okay? This is exactly why I wanted to have this picnic. I mean, here we are in this beautiful little forest with a river beside us—it's June, the sun is out, you're not working on a case right now, and"—she smiled up at him—"we're finally all alone."

"You're right," Frank said, gently wrapping his arms around his girlfriend. "I overreacted—a little. I guess I'm still jumpy from tracking down guerrillas in the jungles of Central America."

A breeze wafted past them, carrying the strong, sweet smell of honeysuckle. "I'm glad you're deciding to wind down, Frank," Callie said. "Sometimes I think you'll never learn how to relax."

Frank chuckled. "You don't need to worry about *that*, Callie."

"I wouldn't dream of doing anything right now," she answered, looking directly into his eyes.

"Next time," Frank whispered, returning her tender gaze, "I'll let you step right into the stuff."

Callie pushed herself away from him. "You really know how to sweet-talk a girl, don't you, Frank Hardy?"

Frank tried to choke back a laugh. "Oh, Callie, come on, I was kidding—"

"Very funny, Frank. I went through all the trouble to make sandwiches, then I found this remote spot fifteen miles from Bayport—"

Just then a loud voice rang out through the woods. "TOOOOO BEEEEEE, . . ."

"What's that?" Frank said.

"And all you can do is make fun of—" Callie suddenly stopped and listened.

"OR NOT TOOOO BEEEE; . . ."

"I don't know," she said. "Sounds like someone reciting poetry."

"THAAAT IS THE QUESTION: . . ."

"No—not poetry," Frank said, frowning as he thought. "It's from *Hamlet*—Act Three, Scene One, where Hamlet considers suicide."

"It's probably some frustrated actor sounding off. Let's see if we can find a quieter spot."

"Actually, that guy's voice sounds kind of strange. What do you think, Callie?"

They listened again to the booming voice.

"TO DIE, TO SLEEEEP—NO MORE! . . ."

"He does sound odd," Callie admitted. "But—"

"Come on, let's check it out," Frank interrupted, eagerly making his way down the hill toward the river. Reluctantly, Callie followed.

"FOR IN THAT SLEEP OF DEATH WHAT DREAMS MAY COME, . . ."

"Now he sounds *really* weird," Callie remarked as they followed a bend in the river.

Just ahead of them, an old wooden bridge drooped over the river. Its supports were cracked, and its rotting floorboards dangled in the air. On either end hung tattered strips of orange tape that had once stretched across the bridge to stop people from crossing.

It seemed that common sense alone would have prevented anyone from stepping onto the bridge—especially with the strong currents of the river below.

Just then Callie and Frank made out a dark figure in the sun's glare. A silver-haired man in black clothing stood in the middle of the bridge, facing away from them.

"FOR WHOOO WOULD BEAR THE WHIPS AND SCORNNNS OF TIIIME, . . ."

"He's a lunatic, Frank!" Callie whispered. "Listen to him!"

Frank picked up his pace as the man raised his arms upward. "I *am* listening. This is the part where Hamlet thinks of ending his life with—"

"WHEN HE HIMSELF MIGHT HIS QUIETUS MAKE WITH—"

"What's he got in his hand?" Callie asked.

"I can't tell—"

"A BARE BODKIN!"

"What's a bare bodkin?"

Frank burst into a sprint toward the bridge. "It's a dagger! This guy's serious!"

Callie immediately shouted, "Don't do it, sir! Everything will be all right!"

Startled, the man spun around to see the two of them running along the riverbank. His face was lined with wrinkles, and despite his look of utter weariness and despair, not a hair was out of place.

"Stay your futile efforts, foolish youths!" the man shouted. "All is lost; my time is at hand!"

With a sweeping gesture, he raised the dagger high and pointed it toward his own chest.

Frank could see there was no time to climb up to the man. He slid into the mud just under the end of the bridge.

"Into the great everlasting I commend my spirit!" the man bellowed, ready to plunge his knife downward.

"Noooooo!" Callie screamed.

At that moment Frank grabbed onto one of the bridge's broken supports and shook it with all his strength. The old bridge creaked and wobbled. Losing his balance, the man reached out with one hand to grab the railing. Splintering planks flew in all directions.

Then, with a *crack* that echoed all along the river, the wooden support gave way. One side of the bridge jerked down, and the man slid feet first on his stomach into the roaring current, his right hand still clutching the dagger.

A bloodcurdling scream sliced the air just before his silvery mane disappeared below the surface. Callie stared in horror as the current carried the man toward her.

"He's heading for the rocks!" she cried.

Gasping and flailing, the man lifted his head out of the water. "Help me! I can't swim!" he managed to sputter.

Instantly, both Frank and Callie dove in after him. The man bobbed up just above and then below the surface. He looked panic-stricken. Fighting the current, they caught up to him. Callie reached for his shoulders—only to be met by the gleaming blade of the dagger as it *whooshed* through the air, inches from her face.

"I can't get near him!" Callie shouted.

"You've got to calm down, sir!" Frank called out. "Just keep your arms still! You'll float long enough for me to bring you in!"

"I—can't—swim—" the man repeated, choking on silt-laden water. Frank realized the man was unable to help; he was blind with fear.

With a powerful lunge, Frank grabbed him around the chest. The man kicked and thrashed even harder, waving the knife in his hand.

"Watch it!" yelled Callie.

Keeping his right arm around the man, Frank reached across and grasped the man's right forearm with his free hand. He jammed his thumb into a pressure point on the wrist and swung the man's arm upward. The dagger flew into the air and plopped into the river ten feet upstream.

By then the man was beginning to lose strength.

As Frank struggled to swim with him, Callie glanced up and was startled to see a line of jagged rocks only fifty feet away.

"You have to let him go, Frank," Callie said. "We'll never get away in time!"

"He's unconscious! Help me out!"

Straining with the effort, Callie swam to Frank and grabbed one of the man's arms. Together, they slowly towed him to the riverbank, narrowly missing the rocks.

They laid the man's limp body on the wet ground. After a minute of Frank's mouth-to-mouth resuscitation, the man suddenly coughed and came to.

"Wha—where—" he sputtered, trying to focus his eyes. "I'm alive, aren't I?"

"You survived without a scratch," Frank said. "Looked like you were having a rough time up there, huh?"

" 'A rough time,' he says," the man muttered. His voice was weak but full of anger. "Oh, callow, fallow youth—you do still believe in the unquestioned perseverance of life at any cost, don't you?"

"Wait a minute," Frank said firmly. "Let's have it slowly, and in English. Who are you, and what were you doing up there?"

"*I* am a troubled man, sir," the stranger answered, throwing back his head in a grand gesture as Callie helped him to sit up. "Tyrone Grant is the name." He dropped his gaze downward and nodded sadly. "Yes, *the* Tyrone Grant of the stage and screen. Don't be shocked."

Hearing nothing but silence from Frank and Callie, he looked up to see their blank stares. "I can see you don't frequent the art movie houses, do you?"

Frank and Callie shook their heads.

"Just as well. I'd shatter your image of me. Now I'd like to ask *you* a question. Just what right do you have in trying to keep me from my task?"

"I don't care what you say, Mr. Grant," Callie said softly, "suicide is never the answer. Think of your family—"

Grant's steel gray eyes bored into Callie. "My family? You must mean that woman I was once married to, who left me for a Hollywood film editor!"

"I-I'm sorry to hear that," Callie said.

"Oh, I haven't even begun yet. There's not much work these days in 'quality' films, you know. I was barely paying the bills with my nonacting job—and now I've lost that, too! What does a man of my age and circumstances have to live for? What? What?" He looked around at the ground. "Where's my dagger?"

"I'm afraid it's in the river, Mr. Grant," Frank said. "Listen, why don't you let us give you a ride home? Maybe you should get some rest, think things over."

"That knife was a Grant family heirloom! I'll

sue! Not only do you rob me of the dignity of killing myself, but you save my life *and* throw away the most treasured possession. . . ."

Callie and Frank looked at each other and rolled their eyes. As they turned to climb the hill, they beckoned Grant to come with them.

Grant complained all the way, but he did follow them up the hill and through the woods to Callie's car. Callie pulled an old wool blanket out of the trunk and gave it to Grant to wrap around himself.

By the time Callie started the car, Grant was sobbing in the back seat.

"Please, Mr. Grant," Callie said. "I'm sure everything will work out. Why don't you tell me your address?"

"Ninety-four Lakeview Avenue!" he answered, brushing away tears with the back of his hand. "And if you insist on preserving my life, you could at least have the courtesy to give me a tissue!"

As Frank handed back a tissue, Callie entered a section of Bayport that was unfamiliar to her. Grant continued to complain as she drove through the outskirts of the city. Just past a bait-and-tackle store was a sharp bend in the road. Callie approached at thirty miles an hour.

"Slow down," Frank whispered. "You're driving too fast!"

Callie braked, gritting her teeth. She didn't usually drive fast, but this time she'd had enough.

Frank and she had risked their lives to save Grant's, and the actor wasn't the least bit grateful.

"And furthermore," Grant said, in a booming voice, "I would appreciate your *not* leaking this to the press!"

Abruptly Callie stopped the car and whirled around to face Grant.

"Mr. Grant!" she said sharply. "I've listened for long enough. Like it or not, we just saved your life. Now will you please . . ." she said, not finishing the thought as she pulled onto the street again.

Grant's face lost all its color as he stared silently past Callie and out the windshield. A minute later Frank grabbed the steering wheel of the car, which was entering a blind turn too quickly. "Callie, pay attention!" Frank shouted.

A blue flatbed truck whizzed around the corner, blowing its horn and just missing them.

"You see what you're making me do, Mr. Grant?" Callie said. They all breathed a sigh of relief, even Tyrone Grant, as Callie slowed the car for the turn.

And suddenly there, in the wrong lane, was a fiery red sports car convertible, hurtling straight toward them!

Chapter

2

"HANG ON!" CALLIE screamed as she yanked the steering wheel far to the right. The car swerved into a guardrail and bounced off, just as the sports car spun away from them, its tires squealing.

Crrrunch! A sickening noise filled the air as Callie pulled her car to a stop on the side of the road. Callie and Frank turned and saw the red car nudged up against a telephone pole.

"Are you all right?" Frank asked.

"Fine," Callie said. "I think we got the better end of the deal."

They both hopped out and ran to the other car. It was only dented in a bit in the front.

"I'm fine, too, you know!" Grant shouted after them. "What's become of your great concern for *my* life?"

As Frank and Callie approached the left door, it flew open. A shrill voice pierced the air:

11

"Why don't you watch where you're driving?" Brushing herself off, a tall redheaded girl of about eighteen climbed out of the car. She adjusted her three gold necklaces and smoothed down the wrinkles on her tight jumpsuit. She shot a poisonous glare at Frank and Callie before putting on her sunglasses. Then she walked over to Frank and Callie. There was something very familiar about her, Frank thought.

"Look what you've done to my Lamborghini!" she cried out. "It's ruined!"

"Well, hardly that. I am awfully sorry about it, though," Callie said. "But I think *you* were the one—"

"Don't try to lay the blame on me! I—"

"Look," Frank interrupted, "the insurance companies will settle it. You have to exchange insurance information. The only important thing now is, how are you?"

The redheaded girl sneered. "I *was* fine until you came along. Now I have to call a cab and call my garage—and I'm late enough as it is!"

She marched back to the driver's seat and pulled a mobile phone out of the car. Frank tried to remember where he'd seen her face before.

"Hello, Harley?" she said into the phone. "Hello? I can't hear you. . . . Yes, it's me. . . . Tessa! . . . Tessa! . . . What? . . ." With a frustrated cry, she threw the phone back in the car.

"It's broken!" she said. "What am I supposed to do now? Walk?"

Fighting an urge to tell her off, Callie said, "Well, my car is okay. Can I give you a ride?"

"Were *you* driving?" the girl asked bitterly.

"Yes."

"I'll go, but only if *he* drives," she said, waving a finger at Frank.

Callie shrugged her shoulders and headed back to her car, giving Frank a look of exasperation as she passed him.

Frank tried to take the girl's arm but she drew away. Throwing back her silky red hair, she walked toward Callie's car.

"By the way," Frank called after her, "aren't you Tessa Carpenter, the one I read about—"

"—in *Personality* magazine," Tessa said sarcastically, finishing Frank's sentence. "Yes, that's me. Ridiculous article, wasn't it? 'Bayport's poor little rich debutante—heiress to the famed Cliffside Mansion and the area's largest art collection . . . but how has she survived the tragic loss of her parents?' " She rolled her eyes. "*Now* I suppose you want to be my best friend, like everyone else."

I wouldn't dream of it, Frank thought to himself as they both climbed into the car. But to Tessa, he just chuckled and said, "No, no, I was just interested in your story. Seems like a huge place for one person to live."

After making her phone calls from a nearby

phone booth, Tessa climbed into the backseat cautiously, as if she were entering a garbage truck. "The Bayport Museum—and fast," she said to Frank.

By this time, Tyrone Grant had curled himself into a ball in his half of the backseat, wrapped from head to toe in the blanket Callie had given him. Tessa peered at him over her sunglasses. "You didn't put me back here with a sick person, did you?"

Grant's only reaction was to shift slightly under the blanket.

"Well, not exactly," Frank said. "He's okay, probably just exhausted. What's happening at the museum? Checking on the Carpenter collection?"

Tessa smirked. "Not checking on it. Taking it back."

"Really?" Frank said. "*Personality* says the collection makes up about half the museum!"

"They're wrong," Tessa answered dryly. "It's about sixty percent. But it all belongs to me now, and I've decided the paintings would spruce up the house."

I wonder what the curator says about this, Frank thought.

He soon found out. As they approached the museum, they noticed a group of five men gathered around a truck at the side of the building. Four of them wore plain gray uniforms and were trying to load large crates onto the truck. The fifth was a stocky man in a dark blue suit and wire-rimmed glasses. As the workmen brought the crates to the truck, the fifth man was shouting and gesturing angrily, his thinning blond hair flopping in front of his reddened face. It appeared that he was trying to keep the men from working.

"This is the last straw," Tessa muttered under her breath. "I have to talk to the fat guy," she said to Frank.

Frank drove up a circular driveway to the side of the museum and Tessa hopped out. "Albert, Albert," she said, shaking her head. "What *are* you doing to these poor men?"

The man wiped his brow with a handkerchief and pushed up his glasses. "Miss Carpenter, may I remind you that this artwork is on *permanent* loan to the museum—as per our agreement with your family, signed thirty years ago by your grandfather! As curator, I cannot let these out of my sight!"

Tessa nodded patiently. "Albert, you yourself said you couldn't find this so-called agreement, remember?"

"You've got to give me some time! After the fire last year, we moved all our old files to the warehouse upstate, and many things got mixed up—"

"Look," Tessa said, continuing, "you've seen a copy of my parents' will. The collection belongs to me now, and I want it back. Besides, don't you think you've had these things long enough? Maybe it's time to redecorate.''

''*Redecorate?* Young lady, we are talking about a museum, not a bedroom! These are priceless paintings and sculptures—the museum is nothing without them!''

Tessa let out a lighthearted laugh. ''Oh, please don't take it so seriously! You should just be glad you had them for so long!''

''Glad we had them! Why, your actions are illegal. Your parents would never have allowed this.''

As the man stammered in shock, one of the workmen tried to push past him. ''Come on, Mr. Ruppenthal, this stuff is heavy. Listen to the girl.''

''Over my dead body,'' Ruppenthal said, shoving the workman back.

Thrown off balance, the workman fell onto the ground. ''Okay, buster,'' he said as he picked himself up, ''if you say so.''

With that, he let loose with an uppercut that caught Ruppenthal squarely in the jaw. After Ruppenthal fell, three museum officials rushed out of the building to come to his aid. One of them sank a fist into the workman's stomach, sending him flying into a crate.

Rubbing his jaw, Ruppenthal yelled, ''Watch it, Felipe! That's the Rodin statue!''

Instantly a melee broke out—workmen against

museum staff. Ruppenthal darted around, trying to move the artwork out of the way.

Frank watched the scene in amazement. "I'm going to try to stop this! You call Joe from the corner pay phone!" he said to Callie, and he ran toward the fight.

He pulled Felipe off one of the workmen. Then he spun around just in time to see another workman running toward him with his fists balled.

"I don't believe we've met," Frank said, extending his right hand. The workman uncorked a haymaker, which Frank easily ducked, sending the man tumbling.

"Ease up, fellas, let's talk this over!" Frank shouted to no avail. A museum worker jumped on him from behind, trying to wrestle him to the ground. But Frank remained upright, lifting the man off his feet and hurling him in the direction of Tessa, who was watching wide-eyed while backing away toward Callie's car.

Within moments came a welcome sound—the high-pitched wail of a police siren. Frank looked up the driveway to see two familiar sights—the patrol car of Officer Con Riley and the Hardy brothers' black van.

"All right, boys, playtime is over!" Officer Riley's voice barked over the patrol car's megaphone. The men all let go of one another and tried to look as nonchalant as possible.

Officer Riley, his partner, and Callie walked up

to the scene. They were followed by Frank's brother Joe, who had hopped out of the van.

"All right, Ruppenthal," Officer Riley said. "What happened here? Does this have to do with the Carpenter items?"

"That's right, Officer," Ruppenthal answered. "These men are forcibly trying to remove this artwork!"

"Or are you 'forcibly' trying to prevent them?" said Officer Riley with a knowing look. "Miss Carpenter already called me about this. I'm afraid that unless you can produce an agreement that says the artwork belongs to you, you'll have to let these men do their job."

"But—but—"

"You can protest all you want in court, my friend. Not here."

As Ruppenthal and Officer Riley argued, Joe joined his brother. He glanced around at the group of burly men, all of whom were now disheveled.

Joe whistled in awe and ran his fingers through his blond hair. "Whew, looks like I missed a big one," he said. "How was it?"

"Fine," said Frank with a smile, massaging a bruised arm. "But we missed you."

With a mischievous grin and a gleam in his blue eyes, Joe moved closer to his brother and said softly, "By the way, who's the redhead in the jumpsuit?"

Frank chuckled. "Believe me, you wouldn't be—"

Suddenly a loud scream ripped through the conversation. All heads turned to the end of the driveway.

There, up against Callie's car, Tessa Carpenter was frozen in fear. Around her neck was a pair of hands. Her body shook as the strangler repeatedly slammed her against the car.

Frank and Joe raced up the driveway, with Callie right behind. "It's Grant!" she cried out in disbelief. "He's trying to kill Tessa!"

Chapter

3

WHILE FRANK WENT to help Tessa, Joe grabbed Grant by his still-soggy collar and pulled him backward. "Tessa, are you okay?" Frank asked.

"I'm—fine," Tessa said with both hands on her throat. "Just a little dizzy."

"I've had enough, Tessa Carpenter!" Grant shouted, gesturing wildly at Tessa. "I had hoped to escape your mocking glance for good! But no—still you torment me!"

Frank slid in front of Tessa, who cowered in fright. Grant tried to lunge for her again, pulling against Joe's tight grip. Within seconds, Officer Riley and his partner arrived. They yanked Grant away and slapped handcuffs on him. Callie and Joe stood by Frank.

"Forgive me, Officer," Grant said, his voice cracking with emotion. "She has forced me to do things I'd never dreamed of!"

When Officer Riley had a good look at Grant,

his face lit up. "Say, aren't you the fella in the new flick? What's it called—*Horror High School III?*"

Grant turned red and looked at the ground. "A cameo role," he said, grimacing.

Frank turned to Tessa. "Sure you're okay?"

Tessa leaned against Frank's broad chest to steady herself. "Yes, I think so," she said faintly. She glanced up at him, her eyes filled with relief and admiration. "Thanks to you."

Joe rubbed his hand. The outline of human teeth—Grant's teeth—was beginning to rise up in a welt. Great, he thought, I get rabies, and Frank walks off with the glory. "It was nothing!" he called out. "We're happy to help you—"

Tessa just looked at him blankly and turned back to Frank. "How can I possibly repay you for saving me from that horrible man—"

"I heard that, Tessa!" Grant called out. "Funny how your opinion of me has changed over the years!"

"Calm down, Mr. Grant," Frank said. He looked back at Tessa. "You *know* this man?"

Tessa gave Grant an icy stare. "You bet I do. And his name isn't Grant either. It's Edwin Squinder. He used to work for my parents—"

"Bless their souls! I don't know how those two marvelous people could have created a monster like her," Squinder said. "For twenty years I was their chauffeur—on call, day and night. But was I unhappy? No! The Carpenters treated me like family! I lived on the grounds of the mansion—even took care of Tessa when she was little. For them, I gladly gave up a promising career in the theater!" He looked squarely into Tessa's eyes. "And in return, they left her money to retain me for life!"

"Your act isn't working, Edwin," Tessa said. She shook her head with scorn and turned to the others. "How could I retain someone who couldn't do his job? Who spent day and night in front of the TV set, imitating actors in old movies?"

"Who refused to drive you to parties on his one night off a week! That's all it was!" Squinder shouted. "A year ago she fired me—and all her other servants—because she's spent almost all her inheritance on clothes, cars, wild parties—"

"Okay, okay, enough of this," Officer Riley said. "Miss, do you want to press charges?"

Squinder suddenly looked frightened. "Please, Tessa. If you have a heart, don't do it. You know I'm not a violent man. I just—flew off the handle. Times have been rough."

Tessa sighed. "No, Officer, I can't be bothered. I think Mr. Squinder will know better than to mess with me again."

Officer Riley looked surprised, but let go of Squinder and unlocked the handcuffs on his wrists. "If you say so."

"Thank you," Squinder said softly. He

brushed himself off, lifted his chin high, and walked away.

"I'm not sure we should let him go," Frank said. "A few hours ago he was about to commit suicide."

Tessa nodded. "I'm not surprised. He does this every few months—but only when he knows people are around to stop him. It's his eccentric way of dealing with his failure as an actor. He's crazy, but harmless."

When Squinder was out of sight, Officer Riley said, "I don't like the looks of him. Be sure to call us right away if there's any more trouble. Frank, I think you or your brother ought to give Miss Carpenter a ride home." With a smile and a wink, he tipped his cap and walked back to the squad car with his partner.

Callie thought she sensed a special meaning behind Officer Riley's wink, and she wasn't so sure she liked it. Especially when she caught a glimpse of the way Tessa was looking at Frank.

"You know, Frank," Tessa said, flashing a warm smile, "you handled Squinder beautifully. And I just couldn't believe how you singlehandedly took on all those men by the truck!"

"It was nothing," Frank mumbled, feeling uncomfortable under Callie's burning gaze.

"Listen," Tessa went on, touching Frank's hand, "I'm having a big party tonight in my house—sort of a celebration for the arrival of the artwork. I'd *love* for you to come!"

Frank cleared his throat and cast a nervous glance at Joe and Callie. "Oh!" Tessa said, following Frank's glance. "You can bring your friends too."

At that, Joe stepped forward with a broad smile and an outstretched hand. "I'm Joe Hardy, Tessa—Frank's brother."

"Nice to meet you," Tessa replied. "And is this your sister?"

Callie looked as though a chill had shot through her. "No," she said dryly, "I'm just the driver."

"This is Callie Shaw," Frank added quickly. "She's—"

Joe could barely contain himself. "We'd be happy to come to your party, Tessa! Listen, I'm free right now. Can I give you a ride home?"

Tessa's smile fell slightly, and she looked over at Frank, as if expecting him to offer her a ride too.

Feeling relieved, Frank said, "Thanks, Joe. I'll go with Callie. See you later." He headed after Callie, who was already walking to her car, while Joe flirted with Tessa on the way to the van.

" 'And is this your sister?' " Callie said, mocking Tessa's voice. "Sorry, Frank, I can't help it, she makes me furious! Did you catch the way she was looking at you?"

Frank put his arm around Callie. "I know," he said. "She's obviously spoiled rotten. But don't worry about me. It's Joe who seems to be falling for her."

Callie took out her keys as Frank went around to the passenger side of her car. "Yeah, but she definitely has her eye on you. Did you see how disappointed she looked when she knew Joe was taking her home?"

"But, Callie, don't you see? It doesn't matter!" They sank into the car's bucket seats, and Frank leaned over to Callie with a glowing smile. "This man has eyes for only one ravishing beauty—you!"

Callie started to put the key in the steering column, but stopped when Frank brought his face closer and gave her a kiss. At that moment, Tessa Carpenter faded from memory.

"I'm sorry, Frank," Callie said. "I guess I'm just upset that our day together had to be spoiled like this."

"I'll make it up to you, Callie, I promise. Next Saturday we'll—"

"I was thinking of something sooner than next Saturday," Callie said eagerly. "Why don't we go see a movie tonight?"

Frank looked at her blankly. "Tonight? Well—we can't."

"Why not?"

"Did you forget? We've been invited to a party."

"Party?" Callie had no idea what he meant. Then it dawned on her. "You mean at Tessa's?"

"Well, yeah!" Frank said with a shrug. "I mean, we agreed. It might be fun—"

Callie's face clouded over. She started the car and pushed her foot down on the accelerator. Frank fell back in his seat.

"Fine," she said, glaring straight ahead. "You go ahead. *I* have other plans."

"Why so glum, chum? This party's going to be the hottest ticket in town!" Joe called out from the bathroom as he stood in front of the mirror, combing his hair.

Frank yanked on good black socks and stared at the bedroom carpet. "I don't know, Joe, I just can't get excited about it." He plopped himself down on the bed and flipped through a copy of *Personality* magazine that Joe had left lying open.

"Well, you won't believe her house." Joe leaned into the room and gestured with his comb. "When I drove her home she told me to go up this narrow road through the woods—only it turned out not to be a road, but her *driveway*! At the end there was this enormous brick mansion— a lawn the size of a football field, servants' cottage, in-ground pool—"

"Hmm. There's a picture of it here in the magazine."

"Right. And that's not even the best part— read the section about the Borgia Dagger," Joe said, walking into the bedroom.

"The what?" Frank flipped through the pages and saw the headline: HEIRESS INHERITS CARPEN-

TER COLLECTION—INCLUDING DEADLY BORGIA
DAGGER!

"Part of that museum collection," explained
Joe, "is a jeweled knife that once belonged to this
sinister Italian family about four hundred years
ago. They were all religious and military leaders,
but they were also cold-blooded murderers! Legend has it that the dagger Tessa has is cursed."

"What kind of curse?"

Joe continued in a low, creepy voice. "The
owner of the dagger will die within a few months
of having touched it." He opened his eyes wide
and let out a deep, diabolical laugh. "Yaaaa-haaa-
haaa-haa—"

Abruptly Joe ducked and just missed being hit
by the rolled-up copy of *Personality* that Frank
had hurled at him.

Approaching the mansion in the dark, even
Frank was impressed. Four pointed spires rose
from the roof like the towers of a castle. A porch,
shrubbery and flower beds surrounded it, and a
rolling lawn stretched far into woods in all directions. There were no other houses visible. Loud
music echoed through the night air and lights
glared from four bay windows on the first floor.

They parked the van and walked inside. Immediately Joe felt that his blue suit wasn't right.
There seemed to be two types of guests: One type
wore expensive tuxedos and evening gowns. The
other type wore more casual clothing, but Joe

could immediately tell it was just as expensive. Standing among them, a wiry man scribbled notes on a small yellow pad.

"Probably a society columnist," Joe whispered to Frank.

"It's Frank and Joe! Come on in!" Tessa's voice floated toward them over the noise of the crowd. From behind a group of laughing people, she emerged.

Frank thought Joe's jaw would drop off. Tessa wore a slinky, full-length gown with silver sequins and high-heeled silver shoes. She grabbed both of their hands and pulled them toward a tall, dimpled guy with dark brown hair. He was about six-foot-one and eighteen years old, same age and height as Frank—only he looked as though he had just stepped out of a movie.

"Frank and Joe Hardy, meet Harley Welles." Harley's teeth were blindingly white as he grinned and said hello.

Next to Harley was a tiny, white-haired woman who looked about fifty years older than anyone else in the room. Her gray-green eyes twinkled behind thick glasses as Tessa introduced her. "And this," Tessa said, "is my very dearest friend, Dr. Harriet Lansdale. I've known her longer than anyone in the world."

Dr. Lansdale's shoulder shook as she chuckled. "That's because I delivered her!" she said. "Welcome to Cliffside Heights. I hope the two of you will come back in the daytime to see the grounds someday. Tessa has lovely gardens.''

"Aunt Harriet is semiretired," Tessa said. "She works only part-time now, at the Cliffside Country Club—the rest of the time she spends gardening. Here and at her own home."

Frank nodded and looked around. They were in a huge parlor, its walls crammed with gold-framed paintings. A towering marble statue of a Greek warrior stretched to the ceiling in a corner between a bookcase and a sideboard.

Just then the doorbell rang. "Harley, be a dear and go into the kitchen for some more cups! Excuse me," Tessa said, and she went to open the door.

"Come and look at the collection," Dr. Lansdale said, leading the way for Frank and Joe to follow. "Personally, I'm trying to convince her to return everything, but we might as well appreciate it while it's here."

Joe looked longingly at the buffet table that stretched across the middle of the room and ended near the Greek statue. They were moving toward the old sideboard.

Three teenagers dressed in fringed leather jackets were standing around a glass case resting on top of the dark carved-wood piece.

"Excuse me, Muffy," Dr. Lansdale said to one of the girls in the group. They parted as the doctor edged up, pointing to the glass case. Inside it, on a purple satin cushion, was a long knife that reflected the light off its gold-and-jeweled handle.

"Here's the centerpiece of the collection," Dr. Lansdale continued, "the Borgia Dagger that you've probably read about."

"Oh, wow, it is incredible!" Muffy said, lifting up the lid of the case and taking out the dagger.

Suddenly a voice bellowed, "See what I mean? Look at that—they think it's a toy!"

Frank and Joe turned to see Albert Ruppenthal rushing across the room, followed by Tessa. Ruppenthal grabbed the dagger from Muffy and put it back on the satin cushion.

"I really didn't mean to interrupt, Miss Carpenter," Ruppenthal said. "I thought I'd come over, apologize, and quietly try to persuade you to give back the collection—but this is outrageous!" He glanced at the dagger, which was now being examined by several other guests. "Do you realize how much that dagger is worth?"

Tessa smiled sweetly. "Of course I do, Albert!" She picked it up, and a hush fell over the room as, carrying it, she sauntered over to the buffet table.

Timidly, one of the teenagers said, "Tessa, remember the curse on that thing! If the owner touches it, it's curtains!"

Tessa threw back her head in defiant laughter. She turned to Ruppenthal, pointing at him with the dagger. "Albert, you look hungry. Would you like an appetizer?"

Ruppenthal's face went white with shock as Tessa sliced into a wedge of cheese with the Borgia Dagger. She stabbed the tip of the blade into the slice she had cut, then walked back to the sideboard and offered the cheese to the curator with a mocking smile.

A split second later the lights went out, and the music cut off in midsong. All the partygoers held their breath in a silence that seemed to last forever.

Then came a crash and a scream—Tessa's scream.

Chapter
4

THE LIGHTS CAME back on, and Frank and Joe stared at the marble statue—or rather, at its pieces on the floor. Part of the sideboard was splintered, and shards from shattered glassware lay all around.

And crouched under the sideboard, the Borgia dagger still in her hand, was Tessa, her face white with shock.

Frank, Joe, and Dr. Lansdale knelt down beside her. "Did the statue hit you?" Joe asked, his voice edged with concern.

Ruppenthal stood gaping over the statue. "Twenty-three hundred years old . . ." he murmured as tears formed in the corners of his eyes.

Tessa was shaking with fright. She looked past Joe and saw Frank. With a choked sob, she let go of the dagger and stood up and threw her arms around him. "Oh, Frank, I was almost killed!"

The crowd started to murmur. Smothered by

Tessa's embrace, Frank said, "Well, you seem to be okay. Why don't you just—uh, sit back and relax a little." As Tessa let go, Frank looked around uncomfortably.

"Mind if someone tells me what's going on here?" a voice said from above.

Frank looked up to see Harley towering over him. This time the glittery smile was gone, replaced by tightly pursed lips.

"Looks to me like an accident," Frank replied.

"I—I can't figure it out, Harley," Tessa said. "There was a blackout, and someone must have knocked over the Roman statue—"

"Greek!" Ruppenthal cried, now sitting on the floor with his head in his hands.

Harley knelt down and helped Tessa over to a sofa, while Joe quietly picked up the dagger and put it back in the glass case, which was mercifully spared.

Dr. Lansdale, who had disappeared, returned with a dampened towel. She sat next to Tessa and put it on her forehead. All around them, guests from the party gathered.

Holding Tessa's hand, Dr. Lansdale smiled and said, "You know, if I were a superstitious person, I'd think this incident was connected to that silly Borgia curse." She looked at the concerned faces around her and chuckled. "And I see I'm not the only one who's thought of it."

Tessa swallowed nervously. Beads of sweat

collected on her brow. "What do you know about the curse, Aunt Harriet?"

"Dear child, I really don't think you ought to worry about it."

"Oh, please," Tessa said. "Maybe if I hear how silly it is, I *won't* worry."

Dr. Lansdale sighed. "Well, if you insist." She sat back and fell silent, as if trying to remember the details. The guests all gathered closer around her.

"I must say it's a rather gruesome tale. The Borgias were one of the wealthiest and most influential families in Italy around the turn of the sixteenth century—and there were bound to be a few black sheep among them." She nodded slowly. "Well, the history books don't record it, but legend says that the worst one, the one whose name caused people to shake with fear, was Armando Borgia. He was a nephew of the duke, and he had an interesting collection in his basement— a collection of bodies."

Joe noticed a shudder run through Tessa. Dr. Lansdale placed her hand on Tessa's and said, "Oh, honey, you look petrified. I didn't mean for this silly old wives' tale to scare you. I'll stop."

"No, go on!" Tessa pleaded. "Maybe if I hear about it, it won't seem so scary."

Joe could see the tension on Tessa's face. He knew it would only be worse if Dr. Lansdale continued. "Maybe you'd better not," he said into her ear.

"It's all right, Joe," Dr. Lansdale answered. "I understand your concern, but sometimes this is the best treatment for fear." She turned back to Tessa. "Now then, this Armando Borgia was supposedly the cruelest landowner in Italy. He purposely charged rents that were outrageous in order to keep the peasants weak and overworked. They wouldn't be able to rebel then. He married several women, only to cast each wife into the street when he tired of her—including Marisol Allegra—a breathtaking Spanish-Italian beauty by all accounts, of noble blood, young, trusting—"

"Tell me about the dagger, Aunt Harriet," Tessa said, shaking.

"Yes, of course. You see, Armando rarely left his palace and gardens—but when he did one day, he was shocked to see the streets full of dirty, homeless beggars. Of course, he was the one who had forced them to live like that because they couldn't afford his rents. But to Armando, they were nothing more than human garbage—garbage to be gotten rid of."

"So he killed them?" Tessa asked.

"One by one," Dr. Lansdale said, "he invited the beggars into the palace. He allowed them to wash up and eat until they could hold no more. Most were tearful with gratitude—and then they were invited to see the wine cellar.

"They never came back up.

"It is said that Armando disposed of each of

them with one quick plunge of his jeweled dagger to the victim's heart. The bodies were stacked neatly in the cellar and left there until the end of the week, when they were buried in a single pauper's grave."

Out of the corner of his eye, Frank noticed the society columnist furiously taking notes.

"No one caught on," Dr. Lansdale said. "All people noticed was that the streets were becoming free of beggars."

Suddenly Dr. Lansdale's voice became softer. All of the guests leaned closer to hear.

"One night, as Armando was half-asleep, his door was pushed open. Thinking it was a servant, he just grumbled and turned over.

"But it wasn't a servant. One of his victims had been lying in the cellar—the knife had just missed her heart—alive. With her last ounce of strength, she had dragged herself up to Armando's bedroom, and found the blood-stained dagger."

"Well, that's ridiculous," Tessa said. "How could she have known where to go? . . ." Tessa cut herself off as she realized the answer.

"That's right, Tessa," Dr. Lansdale said. "The beggar woman was Marisol, one of Armando's wives. Not even Armando had recognized her, so changed was she after having been forced into the street. Poverty and wretchedness had driven her to insanity.

"With the life flowing out of her, Marisol flung

open the bedroom shutters, letting in the light of the full moon. And as she raised the dagger over Armando's bed, she screamed his name so loud they say it shattered the windows in the room."

By now the parlor had become so quiet, Frank could hear the beating of his own heart.

"When a servant found them both slumped on the bed, Armando's eyes were wide with the horror of recognition—and the letter *B* had been drawn on his forehead in blood.

"From that day on, the legend goes, whoever takes possession of the dagger dies mysteriously within four months of having touched it."

Dr. Landsdale shrugged her shoulders and gave a small laugh. "Well, aren't you all grim! Don't you see how absurd the story is? I mean, after all, the museum has had this dagger for decades, and no one has died mysteriously—isn't that so, Mr. Ruppenthal?"

Ruppenthal loosened his collar and looked at the floor. "Well—uh, to tell you the truth, no one ever dared touch it while it was at the museum."

Tessa moved to get off the couch, but swayed dangerously. "Aunt Harriet, would you please show the guests out? I think I'd better stay here," she said.

"Of course, sweetheart. But please don't take this thing so seriously. I hope I haven't made matters worse."

"We'll stay awhile, help with things," Joe said eagerly.

Frank narrowed his eyes at his brother. "Thanks a lot, pal," he murmured.

The first guest to go was Ruppenthal, who stormed off in anger. Dr. Lansdale went to the front door and said goodbye to everyone quietly as they left the mansion.

Frank and Joe helped the hired help carry dishes to the kitchen for a half hour, and when they were done, Tessa was still on the couch, fast asleep. They tiptoed out the front door and onto the porch. "Were you hoping to be hired as a butler or something?" Frank asked.

But Joe was deep in thought. "That was the weirdest story I ever heard," he said.

"Well, something about it smells a little funny to me."

"Like the fact that everything was normal before Ruppenthal got there?"

"Yes. And also how Dr. Lansdale wouldn't stop telling that crazy story, even when she knew Tessa was scared out of her wits."

"Well, I tried to get her to stop—" Joe cut himself short, his eyes focused beyond the side of the house.

"What is it, Joe?"

"Shh. The servants' cottage!"

Frank wheeled around to see a dark figure climbing out of the cottage window. "He's heading toward the front of the house," Frank whispered. "Let's give him a surprise." The brothers quietly sneaked down the front stairs and ducked behind the surrounding bushes.

"Do you think he saw us?" Joe whispered.

"We'll find out soon enough," Frank answered.

He was right. As they carefully peered around the side of the house, they froze.

Inches from their faces was the muzzle of a silver-plated revolver.

"Gentlemen, to what do I owe the pleasure of our meeting?" Stepping out of the shadows, his finger poised over the trigger of the gun, was Edwin Squinder.

Chapter

5

"I WOULDN'T RECOMMEND pulling that trigger," Joe said calmly, his hands in the air.

"Spoken bravely," Squinder said. "Now let me give you *my* recommendation. You had better not say a word to Tess—"

"Who's there?" Tessa's voice called out from above the stairs.

Frank and Joe looked up to the tops of their raised hands. They heard a door open, then Tessa's face appeared over them, peering down from the porch. "What in heaven's—Edwin, put down the gun!"

"Never!" Squinder said. "Never again shall I be a slave to your every whim!"

Harley appeared beside Tessa at the top of the stairs. He rolled his eyes when he saw Squinder. "Ease up, Edwin," he said.

"And as for your snide boyfriend—" Squinder continued.

"We all know how you feel, Edwin," Tessa said patiently. She walked down the stone steps with her hand out. "Now will you give me that before I have you arrested for trespassing and stealing?"

"Stealing?" Squinder answered. "Your father *gave* me this gun, and I was foolish enough to leave it here when I was forced off the premises. I only came back here to reclaim what is rightfully mine!" He pointed the revolver at his head. "The only person this gun was meant to hurt is myself. And this time I will not be foiled in my attempt—"

"Well, it may help if you buy some bullets," Tessa said. "First of all, my father *lent* you that gun, to scare away robbers—it was never loaded. Second, what was once my father's is now mine. Third, you're already on thin ice with the police after this afternoon. So,"—she reached out, with her palm up—"if you please?"

Squinder's eyes darted from side to side.

"Give it to her and go home, Edwin," Harley said, joining them at the foot of the stairs. "You need some rest."

Finally Squinder lowered the revolver. "Very well," he said, his voice trembling, "I shall return to the miserable little flat I have been calling a home—and lie awake thinking of other ways to escape the bitter life to which I have been doomed!"

41

With a grand gesture, he placed the revolver in Tessa's hand and strode away.

As Squinder disappeared down the driveway, Joe said to Tessa, "Will you be all right here alone? We could—"

"She won't be alone," Harley snapped. "Dr. Lansdale and I will stay here tonight. Tomorrow we'll make sure she spends the day relaxing at the club. Tessa will be well taken care of, thank you."

"Okay, fine," Frank said, pulling his brother away from the house. "Good night, Tessa. Thanks for inviting us."

"My pleasure," Tessa called back. "Be sure to come by again, anytime!"

Frank and Joe climbed into the van. "Do you think she really meant that, about coming by anytime?" Joe asked as he started the engine.

"Haven't you had enough of her and her snooty friends, Joe? She's definitely not your type."

"That's not what I mean! I think we have a case here. It's obvious someone has it in for Tessa."

Frank nodded thoughtfully as the van rolled down the driveway. "You're right. And I put Squinder high on the list of suspects. I don't think he's as flaky as he lets on."

"Right. I mean, he's probably the only person who knows where to find the fuse box in order to kill the lights—and I thought his alibi about reclaiming the gun was pretty lame."

"There's only one problem," Frank said. "There must have been two people—one to turn off the lights and the other to push the statue. And I have an idea who the other one is—"

They looked at each other and said at the same time, "Ruppenthal!"

As they drove back to their parents' house, Frank and Joe tossed around a couple of questions: Would Ruppenthal *really* have destroyed a valuable work of art just to scare Tessa? And if Squinder were to blame, why didn't he flee immediately after the incident?

There were far more questions than answers. And although they wouldn't admit it to each other, one thought was nagging at both of them: Maybe it was useless even to wonder. Maybe the curse of the Borgia dagger wasn't an old wives' tale after all.

"I suppose I'll forgive you, Frank," Callie said with a smile. "But for a bright guy, you can be pretty thoughtless sometimes!"

"Guilty as charged," Frank replied. "But I'm changing!" He jumped out of his chair and ran over to his parents' refrigerator. "Can I get you some fruit juice, some leftover ham?"

Callie laughed. "There's enough ham in this room already!"

Frank sat back down at the kitchen table. He

shrugged his shoulders and said, "I may have done a thoughtless thing last night, but you have to admit we stumbled into an interesting case."

"Okay, I admit it! From what you've said, both Squinder and Ruppenthal seem pretty suspicious to me. And I'm not so sure that old woman doctor is as innocent as she sounds."

"With someone like Tessa, you never know how many people might have a grudge against her."

"Well, to be honest, Frank, I really think you should keep your distance. I mean, no one has asked you to do anything, after all. And I have a feeling that hanging around Tessa Carpenter will bring you nothing but trouble."

"Maybe . . ." Frank said absentmindedly.

Just then Joe came into the kitchen. "Oh, hi, Callie! You ready to hit the road, Frank?"

"I think so. Callie just stopped by; we were having a talk."

"Where are you guys going?" Callie asked.

Frank and Joe exchanged glances. "Um, well . . ." Frank said, adjusting his collar. "We thought we'd go to the museum—"

Callie's eyes narrowed. She folded her arms. "I see," she said. "Anything there in particular you wanted to see? Or should I say, any*one*?"

Both Frank and Joe started to speak at once, but Callie cut them off.

"I know, you don't want to mention any names, but the initials are Albert Ruppenthal's, right? You'd rather spend time with this Tessa Carpenter case than with me!''

"That's not it, Callie, really—" Frank said.

Callie smiled. "I know. I'm just giving you grief. I know you won't be satisfied unless you follow up this hunch."

Frank grinned. "I'll make it up to you—why don't we see a movie this evening? Something *you* want to see!"

"Great." As Joe scooted out the door, Callie grabbed Frank's hand and gave it a squeeze. "I *do* feel better after our talk," she whispered. "Thanks."

They all went out the front door, Callie to her car and the brothers to the waiting van.

The Hardys smiled and waved to Callie as she drove away.

"I'm surprised she didn't want to help out," Joe said as soon as Callie was out of sight.

Frank grinned and shook his head. "Not this case. I have a feeling Callie's not *too* concerned about whatever happens to Tessa."

"I guess you're right," Joe said. He put the van in gear. "Next stop, Bayport Museum."

As they approached the museum, the first thing they noticed was that the parking lot was almost totally empty.

"It's open on Sundays, isn't it?" Joe asked.

"Sure is," answered Frank as Joe pulled into a

spot. He looked at his watch. "Eleven-thirty— should be peak business time."

They got out of the van and walked inside. After paying their donations, they went into the main exhibit room.

Immediately, they realized why Ruppenthal had become so upset. Where large paintings had once crowded the walls, there were now rectangles that were still painted the original color— beige. All around these spots the walls had faded to a lighter shade. Glass exhibit cases were half-empty, and a museum guard slept in a chair in the corner.

"It's like a tomb in here," Joe whispered.

"I guess word travels fast," Frank mused. "Looks like the Carpenter Collection really was the backbone of this place."

They both turned when they heard the echo of footsteps in the hallway behind them.

"You can go home, Mr. Harris!" a familiar voice called out. The guard in the corner woke up with a start. "It doesn't look too hopeful. I think I'll close up till—"

Albert Ruppenthal cut himself short as he entered the room. "Well, well, a couple of paying visitors," he said. "Enough income to pay for today's electric bill, perhaps. Or have you been sent by your girlfriend to bring me news of more destroyed artwork?"

"We felt very bad about the statue, Mr. Ruppenthal," Frank said, shaking his head. "Actually, we wondered if we could ask you a few questions about it."

Ruppenthal fell silent for a few moments. His eyes moved from Frank to Joe and back again, as if sizing them up, trying to decide something. Finally he said, "All right, let's talk. I have a few questions for you, too."

Together they walked down the hall and through a door that said Authorized Persons Only. Inside the door was a large office with about six desks. Ruppenthal led Frank and Joe to the other end of the office, where a glass door led to several private offices.

Ushering the brothers into his private office, Ruppenthal immediately closed the door and drew the blinds over the windows.

"Have a seat. Now, I feel funny about doing this, but it seems to me you two are very close to Tessa Carpenter."

"Well, I don't know if *close* is—" Joe began to say.

"Yes, we are," Frank butted in. "I'm Frank Hardy and this is my brother Joe. We were schoolmates with Tessa at school."

Joe gave his brother a puzzled look. "Fine, fine," Ruppenthal said, sounding a bit distracted. "I noticed, too, that she seems to depend on *you* an awful lot, Frank. Softens up a bit when you're around—"

Frank shrugged his shoulders and smiled modestly.

Ruppenthal leaned over his desk, glaring at Frank and Joe. "I'll give it to you straight. This museum is in danger of folding. If we don't have the artwork, people won't come. If we don't have the people, companies and agencies will refuse to fund us. But the main thing is, what Tessa is doing is illegal."

"So you want us to find the agreeement," Joe said.

"No," Ruppenthal said, sitting back in his chair. "I have people looking for it, but I'm afraid it's lost or destroyed. What I have in mind is something much more exciting."

Frank and Joe watched as Ruppenthal reached into his top desk drawer.

"The museum has a small reserve fund," he continued. "It has been building over the years for use in extreme emergency. Until now it hasn't been touched.

"Plainly, what I am saying is, I will make it worth your while to convince Tessa to return the Carpenter Collection. I don't care how you do it."

Slowly he pulled a thick envelope out of the drawer and opened it. Onto the desk fell several stacks of crisp one-hundred dollar bills.

"There's ten thousand dollars. If you agree, all of it will be yours."

Chapter

6

FOR A MOMENT the Hardys just stared at the stacks of money in front of them. Then Frank spoke up.

"Let me get this straight, Mr. Ruppenthal. For ten thousand dollars, you would like the two of us to talk to our friend, wine her and dine her if necessary—and somehow convince her to give back the collection."

"We'd be like spies, in other words," Joe said.

"If you like," Ruppenthal said with a smile.

"And we'd be accepting a bribe," Joe went on.

"Well, I prefer to think of it as payment for services rendered," Ruppenthal replied.

Frank and Joe both leaned back in their seats.

"Are you thinking what I'm thinking?" Joe asked his brother.

Frank nodded seriously. "I think so."

Ruppenthal looked nervous. "There's a lot that a couple of young men can buy with ten thousand dollars," he said, eagerly looking from Frank to Joe. "I'd jump at this if I were your age!"

"Well, we're not the jumping type, Mr. Ruppenthal," Frank said. "No deal."

"Don't tell me—you don't think it's enough, right?" Ruppenthal's face became red with anger. He slapped his hand on his desk. "Greed! You're just like that spoiled little friend of yours. This is a *museum*, not a bank. I have no more to give—"

"You missed the point," Joe said. "It's plenty of money. But you're bribing us to do something illegal. That's not the way we operate."

"Let me tell you about illegal," Ruppenthal said, pointing a finger at Joe. "What Tessa Carpenter has done to me—*that's* illegal!"

"We understand what you're saying, Mr. Ruppenthal," Frank said. "We understand that the museum needs the Carpenter Collection—much more than Tessa does. And I really hope you do find that agreement. If not, I'm afraid the best thing you can do is take your case to court—"

Ruppenthal bolted up from his chair. "Out!" he shouted, pointing to the door. "Take yourselves out of my office! If you think I'm going to spend months in court while that girl destroys everything I've ever worked for, you're crazy!"

Frank and Joe got up and walked toward the door. The slam of Ruppenthal's door echoed like a gunshot as the brothers exited into the hallway.

* * *

"I guess we won't get any information from him," Joe said as he and Frank walked out of the museum, past a row of newspaper vending machines. "Imagine him trying to bribe us. He must be pretty desperate." He sighed. "That *was* a lot of money, though . . ."

"Do I hear some second thoughts?" Frank asked as he put some change into the *Bayport Times* machine and pulled out a Sunday paper. "All I can say is, Ruppenthal is sleazy."

"Yeah, but sleazy enough to try to kill Tessa? And do it by ruining a priceless statue? You saw the look on his face when he saw the thing was shattered, didn't you?"

"It may have been an act, Joe. A sacrifice to remove himself from suspicion. He may either be trying to scare Tessa into giving it all back, or—"

"If there's no more Tessa, the art would have to go back to the museum!"

"Exactly. I think we ought to get home and see if we can dig up anything about Ruppenthal in the crime data base."

They jumped into the van, and Joe steered out of the parking lot. Frank settled in his seat and picked up the newspaper. Instantly his eyes lit on the headline.

"Listen to this, Joe," he said. "It's the lead article: 'Curse or Coincidence? Carpenter Heiress Narrowly Misses Death After Touching Legendary Dagger.' "

"I love a juicy story," Joe said. "Read it to me."

" 'The cream of the area's chic younger set was witness to a bizarre turn of events last night at the Carpenter mansion in the Cliffside Heights section of Bayport. It happened at approximately eleven P.M., under the full moon, and no one who was there is likely to forget . . .' "

"Oh boy, they're really milking it," said Joe.

"Let's see—'Several guests left, convinced that the horrible curse had indeed been brought to life. This opinion was echoed by a distraught Miss Carpenter, who was heard to say, "Am I going to have to live with the threat of death for the rest of my life?" Miss Carpenter agreed to grant the *Times* an exclusive interview today at the Cliffside Country Club—' "

"That wasn't too smart," Joe interrupted. "We've got to convince her to stay away from the press. All we need are reporters tagging along on our investigation!"

"Right," answered Frank. "And if there's a lot of publicity about this Borgia dagger nonsense, who knows what kinds of creeps will be after her—playing tricks, trying to 'cure' the curse, claiming to be descendants of the Borgias—"

"One thing seems a little strange to me. You'd think Tessa would want to keep this whole thing quiet. I mean, for someone so—so—*social,* this kind of thing could make her very unpopular."

Frank thought about that for a minute. "Maybe

so. But I don't think she's the kind of person ever to say no to her name in print."

Joe drove up to the Hardys' rambling old Victorian house on a quiet street lined with maple trees in south Bayport. They parked and ran inside to their computerized crime lab, which also doubled as Frank's bedroom

The sleek computer took up very little space, but it contained the most sophisticated crime-fighting software available.

Frank flicked it on, and Joe pulled up a chair beside him. "Let's see . . ." Frank murmured, "Rubin . . . Ruck . . . Ruggiero . . . Ruppert."

"Nothing," Joe said.

"Well, Ruppenthal's clean—at least so far. Let's try Squinder." He punched a few more keys. "Spivak . . . Spode . . . Squantz . . . ah! Here we are—Squinder!"

Frank and Joe stared intensely at the screen as a short list of information appeared.

Joe read parts of the list out loud: "Shoplifting a can of tuna fish, twenty years ago . . . disturbing the peace with loud speechmaking, eleven years ago . . . assaulting tow-truck operator who tried to remove limo from no-parking zone, two years ago. That's it."

"Doesn't exactly seem like a candidate for murderers' row," Frank said.

Just then their eyes were drawn to the window by the slam of a car door. They looked out to see Fenton Hardy running toward the front door.

"What's up with Dad?" Joe asked.

Within seconds, Fenton was up the stairs and at the door of Frank's room.

"Turn off the computer, boys," he said, breathless. "I just got a police report. I'm on a case myself, but I think *you* might be interested in this one. The report is from the Cliffside Country Club."

"Something about Tessa Carpenter?" Frank asked.

"You'd better get over there right away. She's been shot."

Chapter

7

FRANK AND JOE bolted outside and into the van. With a screech of tires, they sped eastward.

Just past the Entering Cliffside Heights sign, the neighborhood changed dramatically. Neat, suburban houses gave way to a heavily wooded area. Joe hugged the road as it curved sharply.

"I have a feeling this road was built for people who have no reason to hurry," Joe grumbled.

Before long they saw a small, hand-painted sign that said CCC. It pointed up a dirt road to the left.

"Not very flashy, are they?" Joe said as he turned.

"Well, it *is* one of the most exclusive clubs in the state," Frank replied. "I guess they have no need to advertise."

Just up the dirt road was a clearing and a circular driveway. As they approached, a smiling man in a brown uniform stood in their path.

Joe jammed on the brake and the man went around to the driver's side.

"Easy, there," he said. "You're guests of . . . ?"

"Tessa Carpenter," Joe said quickly and gunned the van past the guard. He skidded to a stop in front of the clubhouse, a three-story stone mansion surrounded by lavish flower gardens.

As they parked and jumped out, they heard the guard's voice behind them: "Wait! You can't visit her now! Come back here!"

The brothers heard voices and followed them around the building to a large, open meadow surrounded by trees. In the middle of the field was a crowd of people, some of them police officers. Near this group a jittery horse was being calmed by a man in jeans. And circling around the crowd, taking notes, was the same society columnist they had seen at Tessa's party.

"Excuse us," Frank said repeatedly as he and Joe worked their way to the center of the crowd. There they saw Tessa, lying on the ground and sobbing. Kneeling beside her, Dr. Lansdale and Harley were swabbing her bloody forehead with a damp cloth.

"Is she all right?" Joe asked.

Harley barely looked up; he said nothing. But Dr. Lansdale smiled cheerfully. "Ah, hello, Frank and Joe! I had no idea you were members," she said. "I'm afraid Tessa had a rather scary fall. Nothing more than a scraped forehead, fortunately.''

"There's more to the story than that," Harley said. "Somebody tried to kill her."

"I don't know what happened," Tessa said, speaking with the loud, shaky voice of someone who has just had the scare of a lifetime. "I was j-just riding my horse—th-that interview had gotten me so upset and I needed to relax—and—and then I heard it—the shot."

"Were you hit?" asked Frank.

"N-no, but my horse got so upset he—he reared up on his hind legs and threw me off!"

"Could you see who did it?" Joe asked.

"No! I told the police—"

Tessa was interrupted by a scream in the distance.

All eyes turned toward a commotion in the woods. Three police officers, two men and a woman, were emerging. One of the men carried a silver-plated revolver. The other two officers were dragging a kicking teenager.

"It's Callie!" Joe said.

"Impossible," whispered Frank, frozen in disbelief.

"Get those handcuffs away from me!" they heard her scream. "Don't you understand? I'm on *your* side!"

"Sure, kid," answered the policewoman. "You just happened to be illegally trespassing in the woods with a gun when it went off, right? And now you can't help but resist arrest."

Callie's eyes lit up when she saw Frank and Joe.

"Tell them who I am, Frank!"

The policewoman did a double-take. "Well, if it isn't the Hardy brothers," she said, smirking. "Is this one of your strange detective methods?"

"It's okay, Officer Novack. She's—uh, part of our investigation team," Frank said.

"That's what she told us," the policewoman said as Callie defiantly threw aside the two officers' arms and brushed herself off.

Suddenly two country club guards pushed their way through the crowd. "There they are!" one of them yelled. "They just drove past me! Seize them, officers!"

By now the crowd was buzzing with confusion. "All right, let's go back to our businesses," Officer Novack said, loudly. "Ms. Carpenter is unhurt, and these three young people are private detectives."

One by one, the club members began to drift away. "Thanks, Officer Novack," Frank said a little while later.

"Well, we've gotten our report. Ms. Shaw claims that she found the gun in the woods while keeping an eye on Ms. Carpenter. At this point all we can do is take the gun to headquarters for analysis. But you can be sure we'll be in touch— especially with you, young lady." She shot a look at Callie. "If your story doesn't hold up, you'll be brought in for questioning."

As the officers walked toward their squad cars in the parking lot, Frank leaned down to Tessa. "All right, now you know who we really are. We'd like to help you out, since it looks as though one or two people are after your life—"

Tessa flung her arms around Frank. "Oh, I *knew* you were in some line of work like this. I'm so glad."

Frank uneasily pulled himself away and said, "We'll need access to your house, first of all—"

"I have a perfect solution," Tessa answered. "Be my bodyguards, both of you." Frank and Joe were silent. "I have the money to pay you. Don't you see? I need protection, and this way the two of you can pick up all kinds of clues. You'll live on the mansion grounds, in the servants' cottage!"

At that suggestion, Callie looked as if she could kill.

"Uh—we'll think about it," Frank said.

"The only thing to worry about now is how to get you inside to my office so I can take care of you," Dr. Lansdale said.

Joe, Harley, and Dr. Lansdale helped Tessa up and supported her as she walked toward the clubhouse. Frank and Callie followed a few yards behind.

"She won't stop at anything to get her hands on you," Callie said to Frank.

"Wait a minute! First things first," Frank said. "Just what *were* you doing in the woods, anyway?"

Callie looked away. "After you and Joe left for the museum, I got a paper and read that Tessa was going to be here today. So I decided to tail her and—well, investigate!"

"Investigate? Look, Callie—Joe and I are the pros. You can't do this on your own!"

"Well, I don't agree! After all, there should be *someone* on this case who isn't in love with Tessa!" She gave Frank an accusing look. "Anyway, I sneaked over a fence and into the woods. As I was looking for the clubhouse, I heard a horse galloping along a dirt pathway. Sure enough, it was Tessa. I watched her ride into the field, when all of a sudden there was this gunshot. I could tell Tessa wasn't hit, because the shot had come from farther down in the woods. But by the time I got there, there was no one—only that silver-plated revolver."

"Just like the one in Squinder's old cottage," Frank said.

By now they had caught up to the others. Dr. Lansdale was pointing to a spot in one of the gardens. A large patch of soil had been turned over, and hoses, bottles, and seed packets littered the ground.

"I think the arsenic has finally gotten rid of the weeds, Tessa," she said. "And I may actually plant some tomatoes this year!"

"That's great, Aunt Harriet, but I really need to lie down!" Tessa whined.

They continued walking into the clubhouse. Dr. Lansdale led them into her ground-floor office, a modest room with a sink, a chair, a desk, a cot, and several shelves full of supplies.

Tessa moaned as she was set down on the cot. "Oh! My head is killing me!"

"Well, you should have picked a softer place to land, sweetheart!" Dr. Lansdale said with a small laugh. "Here, let me get you a mild painkiller."

Dr. Lansdale reached for a clear plastic bottle on one of the shelves.

"That's it, just relax," she said, not looking as she took a couple of pills out. "These will do the trick temporarily. Harley, be a dear and get a glass of water for Tessa."

Joe looked around the room. Harley was filling a huge glass of water. Frank was propping pillows behind her head. And Callie seemed disgusted with the whole situation.

Just then something caught Joe's eye. Just as Tessa was about to put the pills in her mouth, he picked up the bottle.

His eyes popped open as he read the label: Arsenic!

Chapter

8

THERE WAS NO time for words. Joe leapt across the room and swiped at Tessa's arm. The pills went flying into the air and fell harmlessly to the ground.

Tessa shrieked as Joe hit her arm. Instantly Joe felt a hand at the back of his collar.

"Just what do you think you're doing, pal?" Harley said. He drew back a fist.

"Saving her life," Joe said. He held out the arsenic for everyone to see.

The room fell silent, except for a gasp from Tessa.

"I don't believe it," she said finally, her face as white as the sheet on her cot.

"Oh, my word!" Dr. Lansdale exclaimed, taking the bottle from Joe. "How could I have done this?"

"What's a bottle of arsenic doing in here anyway?" Frank asked.

"My goodness, my goodness, what indeed?" Dr. Lansdale said, shaking her head. "I have told myself time and again that something like this might happen. I buy these from a drug company and then dissolve them in water to use as a weed-killer. I sometimes store them in here. And with my eyesight the way it's gotten these days . . . Oh, honey, how can you ever forgive me?"

"I-it's not you, Aunt Harriet," Tessa said, with tears welling in her eyes. "There's something else in control here, something bigger than all of us."

"Whatever do you mean, sweetheart?" Dr. Lansdale said.

"It's the Borgia curse, I know it!" Tessa was practically screaming by now. "I'm doomed! There's no place I can be safe!"

"Shh, it's all going to be okay," said Frank. "It was a simple accident. There are no such things as ancient curses. This is the twentieth century."

"The boy is right, darling," Dr. Lansdale said. "I'm so, so sorry. From now on I will never make such a careless mistake. I think the best thing for your nerves right now would be a nice, long nap."

She delicately helped Tessa lie back and popped a pillow under her head. "Tha-a-t's it. Harley and I will be here to watch over you, while I ask our guests to leave, okay?"

Almost immediately Tessa's eyes began to flutter shut from nervous exhaustion. Frank, Joe, and Callie tiptoed out the office door, waving goodbye to Dr. Lansdale and Harley.

"I'm sorry, I just don't trust her," Callie said as they walked out of the clubhouse. "The old-lady routine is too convenient. After all, she's a *professional*—a doctor would never do anything like that!"

"I don't know, Callie," Joe said. "She seemed so upset. Besides, she must be pushing seventy or seventy-five. I really think she's a little forgetful and careless."

"Besides," Frank added, "if she were really after Tessa, wouldn't it be a little obvious to knock her off in front of four witnesses?"

"I guess you're right," Callie said with a pout. "After all, *you're* the detectives. Well, now I've got to go rescue my car from its hiding place. I didn't have the *skill* to just drive right up like you did."

As she turned away, Frank could tell that she was only half joking. It seemed to him that Callie was not only jealous, but determined to crack this case herself. Joe and he could certainly use her sharp instincts; if only they could all work together.

"Listen," said Joe, interrupting his brother's thoughts. "What do you think of this bodyguard idea? It seems perfect to me."

Frank nodded. "I'm afraid I agree with you this time, Joe. We're going to need a lot of close contact—"

"I heard that!" came a voice from around a corner of the clubhouse. Callie came storming back toward them. "Close contact? I *know* what kind of close contact you want! I can't believe you're actually falling for her offer!"

Frank exhaled with frustration. "And I can't believe you were actually eavesdropping. Besides, you yourself said it was a fascinating case!"

"It's the victim who's fascinating to you, Frank—the poor little glamorous redhead! You're going to become her slaves, just like Squinder! And, by the way," Callie added, her eyes blazing, "I wasn't eavesdropping; I came back to see what time we were going to the movies tonight. But you can forget that now!" With that, she stalked away.

"Do I detect a note of anger?" Joe said with a wry grin. "Maybe you should drop the case. Then Callie will go to the movies with you tonight, and *I'll* be Tessa's bodyguard."

Frank raised an eyebrow at his brother. "All I can say is, if I manage to crack this case *and* keep my girlfriend, I'll take you both out to the movies—every day for a month."

Frank and Joe lurched to the left as the van took a sharp curve at forty miles an hour.

"Hasn't she learned her lesson yet?" said Frank. "She's going to ruin *that* car too!"

Joe kept the little blue convertible within his

sight as it raced along Cliffside Road. A long mane of scarlet hair billowed back from the driver's seat.

"Can you believe that incredible machine is her *second* car, Frank?"

"Well, I hope her third is a Model T. They only go twenty miles an hour." Frank reached out to steady himself as the van sped over a bump in the road. "We could have offered to drive her home from the club."

"I know, but when I called her from our house, she insisted she was well enough to drive!"

The setting sun washed the woods in an orange glow as the two vehicles approached the Carpenter mansion. In a cloud of dust, the convertible stormed up the winding dirt driveway and skidded to a stop in front of the four-car garage.

Covered with a thin film of dirt, the Hardy van followed slowly behind, its windshield washer squirting away.

"Mom and Dad have Tessa's phone number—right, Joe?"

"Yeah," Joe replied. "And if they need to find us, it shouldn't be hard. Tessa's mansion has been mentioned in all the newspapers this week."

"How did I ever let you sucker me into this bodyguard idea, anyway?" Frank asked as they pulled up behind Tessa's car.

"Me? Wait a minute—"

"Welcome home!" Tessa chirped, standing beside her car.

"Uh, Tessa—" Frank began.

"I can't believe how much better I feel after that nice, long nap!" Tessa went on. "Now, do you need help getting settled in the cottage?" They shook their heads.

She pulled open the van door and skipped away toward the house.

"Amazing how fast she bounces back," Frank said as he and Joe stepped out of the van.

They wandered through the mansion, until they found Tessa rewinding a cassette in a telephone answering machine in the sitting room.

"I love these things," she said. "So much better than secretaries. They don't make mistakes or take lunch breaks—and they're much cheaper."

Beep. There was only one message: "Hello, Miss Carpenter. Albert Ruppenthal here. Just wanted to let you know, the staff in our upstate warehouse has located your grandfather's agreement. It was buried in some files that had been transferred there after the museum fire. I'm expecting it to be brought here late tomorrow, and I expect you to be home Tuesday when we pick up the collection. You will, of course, be responsible for the cost of the Greek statue. Have a pleasant day."

Tessa sank into a leather armchair. Her rosy complexion had quickly become chalky white.

"This was bound to happen," Joe said gently.

He felt sorry for her; she looked more upset than he had expected.

"Bound to happen! That's easy for you to say!" Tessa snapped.

"Sorry, Tessa," Joe answered. "I didn't mean it to sound—"

"I know, I know," Tessa said with a sigh. "Maybe it's just as well anyway. This stupid art collection has caused me nothing but trouble." She looked around at the paintings on the sitting-room wall. "Besides, most of the paintings don't even go with the wallpaper."

"Even when you return the collection, there's still the small matter of our investigation," Frank said.

Tessa snapped out of her gloom. "Right!" she said, looking at Frank with adoring eyes. "What comes next?"

"Well, I will have to check out the parlor, and Joe—"

"No!" Tessa interrupted.

"What's the matter?" Frank said.

Tessa's bottom lip jutted out in a pout. She gave Frank a hurt look and said, "You're not going to leave me alone, Frank? I thought you were my bodyguard."

"Uh—yeah, Tessa. That's right." He looked at Joe and shrugged. "I guess that leaves you to search the house for clues."

"I guess so," Joe said listlessly. He nodded

slowly, walking out the door. "Only who's going to guard you from her?" he muttered.

"What?" Frank called out.

"Never mind," Joe answered as he went through the door.

The Borgia dagger was in its glass case on top of the broken sideboard still. Joe lifted the glass case carefully and saw the carved-oak wall through the case. Was there anything unusual? he wondered—any electrical switches, bugging devices? . . .

He opened the case, lifted the dagger, and peeked under the satin cushion. Nothing. He put it down and then looked in the corner where the statue had been. No mechanical tripping devices.

Maybe there was something in the room he wasn't seeing—a box of circuit breakers, a hidden TV camera—

He stood in the corner and leaned back against the oak wall, surveying the room. His elbow bumped against one of the intricate carvings—and it moved!

He sprang forward. The carving popped back to its original position.

Creeeak! A sudden vibration at his side caught Joe's attention. As he watched in surprise, one entire section of the bookcase swung slowly out of the wall, sending several books toppling onto the floor.

He grabbed the bookcase and pulled it out

farther into the room. Behind it was nothing but pitch-darkness.

A secret room, Joe thought. Just like the old movies. Now we're getting someplace.

With great caution, he took one step into the unknown—and fell straight down through broken cobwebs into a black abyss.

Chapter

9

HE HIT THE cement floor hard. For a moment he lay there, the wind knocked out of him. He flexed his arms and legs. Nothing broken.

Gradually his eyes adjusted to the darkness. He looked around him. A weak shaft of light spilled in from the opening he'd just fallen through. All it enabled him to see was the large, empty room he was in. On the far wall there was a low, open doorway.

He picked himself up and cautiously walked to this other doorway. To enter it, he had to stoop. Stepping carefully, he passed through. He reached out with both hands and felt rough plaster walls on either side of him. The ceiling scraped against his head. The absolute blackness in the tunnel gave him no clue as to his destination—except that he was moving on a sharp downward slope.

Guiding himself with his hands, he groped

along, slowly at first and then picked up speed. This has to lead to something, he thought. A storage room, a boiler room . . .

Thunk. Before he could finish his thought, Joe had crashed into something. He rubbed his forehead where it had made contact with the object. With his other hand, he reached out and felt a wooden door that had blocked his path. He found the doorknob and pushed the door open.

Another dark room. Joe stepped inside—onto a small object that rolled out from beneath him.

"Who-o-oa!" he called out, clutching at the doorjamb, next to which he felt the cool metal plate of a light switch.

He flicked on the switch. The room was flooded with fluorescent light. As Joe's eyes adjusted, he saw trunks, boxes, garden equipment, and a floor cluttered with small objects, including the metal roller skate that he had just tripped over.

On the near wall was something he had hoped to find—a metal panel of circuit breakers. He opened the front of the metal box, and saw about twenty switches. He read the labels beneath each one: Kitchen, Sitting Room, Parlor . . . Below them all was a large, main switch. "Now we're cooking," he said to himself. This was the place where all the lights in the mansion could have been blacked out.

On the far wall were a few rickety wooden stairs that led up to two overhead cellar doors. Now Joe knew where he was. The tunnel had gradually led him down to the basement. He turned back and closed the circuit breaker box, climbed two of the four stairs, and pushed up to open one of the bulkhead doors.

The smell of fresh flowers wafted down to him. Joe stuck his head out into the sunlight.

He looked up and behind him to see the side of the Carpenter mansion. A flower garden stretched to the ends of the house on either side of him, and directly in front of him was a well-worn dirt path.

A dirt path that led directly to the servants' cottage.

A smile flickered across Joe's face. He jumped outside and ran around to the front of the mansion.

As he passed under the window of the sitting room, he heard Tessa's voice:

"Why don't you let me give you a massage, Frank. It will loosen you up. Being my bodyguard hasn't exactly been relaxing so far."

Joe looked through the window to see Frank sitting nervously on the edge of the couch. Tessa was standing behind him and reaching for his neck.

Frank shot up off the couch as Tessa's fingers made contact. "Uh, how about a walk in the— Joe!" he cried, spotting his brother outside. "What are you doing out there?"

"I hope I'm not interrupting anything," Joe replied.

"No, no, come on in!"

Joe trotted around to the front door and then into the sitting room.

"Where have you been?" Frank asked. "We missed you!"

Out of the corner of his eye, Joe caught a glimpse of Tessa, slumped in an armchair, pouting.

"Well, at least one of you did," Joe said under his breath. "But never mind. I think we may have a breakthrough in the case. Tessa, do you have a flashlight?"

"Sure. Do you want me to get it for you?" Joe nodded. Barely hiding her annoyed look, she left the room and quickly returned with a large green flashlight.

"Okay, follow me!" Joe said. He led Frank and Tessa into the parlor. Tessa's jaw dropped as Joe walked over to the section of the bookcase that was swung away from the wall.

"There's a room down here," Joe explained. He pointed the flashlight into the void. "But you have to jump a couple of steps to get to it."

He circled the flashlight around, examining the dark room. Off to the side of the opening, a short metal ladder was leaning against the wall.

"It all makes sense now," Joe said. "There's a tunnel that leads down from this room into a storage area that houses the circuit breakers. Whoever tried to kill Tessa could have used that route to come up here"—he turned toward the

corner of the parlor at their immediate right—
"and then walked two steps into that corner to
shove the statue over."

"Amazing," Tessa said.

Frank nodded his head thoughtfully. "It could
have been only one person then, instead of two."

"Yeah, a real speed demon," Joe said. "He'd
have had to kill the lights, run through the basement in the dark, climb up the ladder, push the
bookcase back into place, topple the statue, and
then go back to turn on the lights again."

"Someone who knows the house backward and
forward—"

"And in the dark," Joe added. He turned to
Tessa. "You knew nothing about this fake bookcase?"

She folded her arms in front of her. "If I did,
don't you think I would have said something,
Joe?"

Joe gave her an embarrassed look. "Well, it is
your house, Tessa."

"This whole thing is giving me the creeps,"
Tessa said. "Secret passageways, moving book-
cases—I feel like I'm in a haunted house! Tomorrow I'm going to call someone to put a wall up
behind that bookcase. I've had enough—"

Frank touched Tessa's arm. "There's nothing
to worry about," he said. "I'd prefer it if you just
left it all alone for a while. We may pick up more
clues."

Tessa backed down instantly when she heard

Frank's voice. "Well, all right, if you say so," she said softly. Just then her eyelids drooped and she raised her hand to her mouth, trying to stifle a yawn.

"You look exhausted," Frank said. "Why don't we continue this tomorrow?"

Tessa nodded. "You're right, Frank. I think I'd better turn in. Sorry, guys. There should be some towels and sheets in the cottage. See you in the morning."

As Tessa went upstairs, Frank and Joe made sure all of the first-floor windows were locked shut. Then they went outside and secured the locks to all the house's entrances and then got their bags out of the van.

"How do you do it, Frank?" Joe asked as they walked toward the cottage. "She listens to every word you say and treats me like Jack the Ripper."

Frank rolled his eyes. "Don't get hung up on her, Joe. She's already got a boyfriend, remember? Besides we're here to solve a case."

"Yeah, you're right, as usual," Joe said with a sigh. Then his eyes narrowed. "Anyway, I think I have an idea who did it."

"I guess we can rule out both Ruppenthal and Lansdale, since they were actually in the parlor the whole time the attempt occurred."

"Not necessarily." Joe stopped in front of the cottage and looked back at the mansion. "Do you see what I see?"

Frank scratched his head. "A dirt pathway that goes from the cottage to the house. So?"

"Who did we see sneaking around the cottage after the party?"

"Of course—Squinder! Squinder might have tripped the lights to help anyone inside the room. Like Ruppenthal or Dr. Lansdale—"

"Or both." Joe gave his brother a knowing look as he opened the front door of the cottage. "Looks like we'll have to pay Edwin a visit tomorrow."

Eighty-five degrees. Joe had to rub his eyes twice before he believed the temperature on the outdoor thermometer.

"It's only eight in the morning!" he said. "Today will be a scorcher."

The Hardys quickly put on shorts and T-shirts, then headed for the mansion. By the time they got there, Tessa was already heading out, dressed in a white terrycloth robe.

"Good morning!" she sang. "I was just coming out to ask if you wanted to join me in a morning swim!"

"Swim?" Joe said. "Uh—we didn't bring—"

"Bathing suits? Don't worry. The room on the side of the cottage is a changing room. We keep extra suits there for guests."

"Thanks," Frank said, "but I think we'd better continue—"

"Sure we'll join you!" Joe interrupted, nudging Frank in the ribs.

"Great!" Tessa said. "You go ahead and change while I call Harley. He loves to swim in the morning."

As Tessa went inside to call, Frank and Joe headed back toward the cottage. They were passing beside the sitting room window when a sharpness in Tessa's voice made them halt in their tracks.

"Don't be a child, Harley! . . . Of course not. . . . I can't believe you're being so jealous. . . . Well, I'm calling *you,* aren't I?"

Frank and Joe glanced at each other. "I think we're creating a problem," Frank said.

Joe nodded, then shrugged his shoulders. "We could use Harley on our side, but it looks as though it's a little late for that. Come on, I'll race you to the changing room." The brothers dashed back to the cottage. "Last one in has to interrogate Squinder!" Joe said, already slipping out of his clothes.

But it was Frank who emerged first, running for the diving board. Joe followed behind him in a pair of baggy plaid trunks, trying to pull the drawstring tight.

Frank ran down the diving board and took a jump. Bouncing down onto the board, he prepared for the dive.

It was in that split-second he saw the thin

electrical wire on the bottom of the pool. Instantly his eyes followed it to an outdoor socket.

With every ounce of muscular control he had, he stopped himself from diving and jumped back down onto the board. Behind him was the sound of Joe's feet slapping the outdoor tiles.

He shouted in a voice so loud he thought his lungs would rip, *"Joe! Don't jump!"*

But it was too late. With horror, he watched his brother plunge into the clear blue water.

Chapter

10

THHHHHWOPP! STILL CLUTCHING the drawstring on his shorts, Joe did a belly-flop into the pool.

That image froze in Frank's mind—it would be the final image he had of his brother.

"NOOOOOOO!" Feeling more helpless than he had ever felt in his life, Frank let out a cry from the bottom of his soul. It seemed as though his mouth was the only part of his body that could move.

There were a few seconds of eerie silence as Joe floated to the surface. Frank couldn't help but turn away from the pool. He had seen some gruesome things in his life, but the sight of his brother's electrocuted body would be too much to bear.

"What? Too much glare from the water? Come on in!"

Was it a hallucination? The voice sounded exactly like Joe's. Frank spun around and looked into the pool, as a sheet of water hit him squarely in the face.

Frank did a double take. There, treading water, was Joe.

"Don't look so shocked. It was only a belly-flop!" he called out.

Frank's face broke into a broad grin. Immediately he ran around to the side and pulled the wire out of the pool—and out of the socket.

"Pretty lucky, huh?" Joe called out. "It must be dead."

"I have a feeling whoever put this here had something else in mind," said Frank.

Just then Tessa scampered down to the pool area in a bright red- and orange-striped one-piece bathing suit. "Hey, why didn't you wait for me?"

Joe shielded his eyes. "I didn't want to be blinded by the suit before I went in!"

"Very funny." Tessa gasped as she saw Frank. "Frank, what are you doing with that wire?"

"It was in the pool. It must have been put in overnight."

Tessa's face turned white. "By someone who knew I take morning swims." She swallowed nervously and steadied herself against a pool chair, her arms shaking. "I—I can't believe this. Why would anyone want to do this to me?"

"Well, we don't know that, Tessa. But we think Squinder may be a major player here."

Suddenly Tessa grabbed Frank's hand. "Are

you all right?" she said. "You didn't get a shock or anything, did you?"

What about me? Joe thought. I'm the one who jumped in.

"Fortunately, no," Frank said. "Even though it was plugged into that outlet." He pointed to the socket by the side of the pool.

"Aren't you lucky!" Tessa exclaimed with a sigh of relief. "That hasn't worked in years. Thank goodness my dad never had it fixed!"

"I think we'd better take a rain check on this swim," said Frank. "We've got to start tailing Squinder."

Tessa shook her head. "I just can't believe it. I know he hates me, but he'd *never* do anything like this."

"Maybe you'd like to come with us and confront him."

"No way! I don't want to go near him anymore."

"In that case," Joe said, climbing out of the pool, "why don't I stay here to guard Tessa while you go, Frank?"

"Yeah, good idea, Joe," Frank said. "In fact, I think I'll call Callie. She can help me follow Squinder."

Joe disappeared into the changing room as Frank went to the cottage to call Callie. After she agreed to meet him at Squinder's house, he reminded her of the address, and he threw on his clothes and jogged out to the driveway.

"So long, Tessa!" Frank yelled as he jumped into the van.

"Oh! Just a minute!" she called out. Tessa ran toward Frank with her arms outstretched. Frank leaned out the window, and she gave him a loud kiss on the cheek.

"I just wanted to thank you for caring about me so much. Good luck." With that, she wrapped her arms around his neck.

Frank sighed with relief as she let go. Then he became aware of a car pulling up behind him. He turned to look. A feeling of dread washed over him when the car pulled up beside him.

Staring at him through the passenger window was an angry Harley Welles.

"Um, morning, Harley," Frank said. "Sure is a hot one, huh?"

With a wave of his hand, he sped down the driveway.

Squinder lived in a section of Bayport only four miles from Cliffside Heights, but it seemed light-years away. Old two-family houses stood side by side with run-down apartment buildings. Tiny front lawns had become nothing but dirt with stray patches of weeds. Except for the squeals of children and the barking of stray dogs, everything was silent and still in the hot summer air. On porches and in open windows, people stared into the distance, lazily fanning themselves. As Frank drove by, they gave him hard unseeing looks.

He made a right up Lakeview Avenue and looked for number 94. Up the street about half a block was a row of attached houses. Callie's car was parked in front of the last one. As Frank approached, Callie jumped out of her car, waving to him.

He parked his car and hopped out. "What took you so long?" she said. "I don't like waiting."

"I had a longer drive than you," Frank answered.

"How's Tessa?" Callie asked, raising an eyebrow.

"I'm sure she's in her glory right now. She's got both Harley and Joe fighting for her attention."

"Good! That leaves you and me to bust this case wide open!" She grabbed Frank's hand and pulled him toward the house marked 94.

"Hey, just a minute. You have to promise me you won't go sneaking off on your own again just to show us up."

Callie put an innocent look on her face. "Me? I wouldn't *dream* of it! Scout's honor!" She raised three fingers.

"Okay, partner, let's go."

Ninety-four Lakeview Avenue was a small, brown house in dire need of a paint job. Just below the roof, some of the siding had fallen off. A battered cyclone fence enclosed the tiny front yard, which hadn't seen grass in years.

Hanging on the fence was a rusted metal sign. Frank squatted down next to it.

"Can you read it?" asked Callie as she pushed open the front gate.

"Not really. It's all covered with graffiti. No, wait a second, I can make out—"

"Never mind, Frank. Look, there's a note taped to Squinder's door!"

"Bo—ware—No, that's beware—of—"

"Beware of what?" asked Callie, halfway to the front door.

"D-dog! *Dog!* Look out, Callie!"

Callie froze as she heard a deep growling and a rhythmic jingling sound. Before she could react, a huge black animal came barreling around the house.

Thinking fast, Frank picked up a stick from the ground. He ran through the gate and stopped in front of Callie, holding the stick high over his head.

"Don't even try it!" Frank shouted. The dog stopped short, baring its huge white teeth.

Frank slowly approached the dog, threatening it with the stick. The dog barked furiously as it backed away.

"Go ahead, Callie! I'll hold him off while you try the front door!"

"Are you sure?"

"No problem! I've got him in control!" Frank hoped he was telling the truth.

Timidly, Callie walked toward the door. As she moved, though, the dog lunged.

Whack! Frank slammed the stick down in the dog's path. The dog backed off, and Frank lifted the stick into the air again. The dog's eyes followed the stick, and it braced itself as if to run.

This is interesting, Frank thought. He began waving the stick slowly in the air. The dog's tail began to wag. Then Frank jerked the stick suddenly to one side, and the dog practically leapt off the ground in the same direction.

"Careful, Frank!" Callie called to him. "It might be part Doberman, or German shepherd—"

"Or retriever!" Frank shouted. He flung the branch clear across the street. Like a shot, the dog darted across after it.

Frank ran to the gate and slammed it shut. He turned to Callie and wiped his hands. "Luckily, that dog is all teeth and no brains!"

Together, Frank and Callie read the scrawled handwriting on the yellow sheet taped to the door:

Dear Simon,
Am at mall, fourth floor. There may actually be a shooting today. See you at 6.
T. G.

"This guy is stupider than I thought," Frank said. "How could he leave a more obvious clue?"

"Come on! Let's catch him before he kills somebody!" Callie raced to the front gate, only to stop short.

Waiting on the other side of the gate, the branch clenched between its teeth, was the black dog. "Uh, why don't you go first, Frank? It seems to like you more," Callie suggested.

Frank opened the gate and let the dog in. Quickly Callie scooted out to her car. Then Frank pulled the branch from the dog's mouth and tossed it up to the front door of the house. As the dog tore away, Frank shut the gate and jumped into the van.

Callie followed Frank to the Bayport Mall. They parked in the indoor lot and ran toward the mall elevator, just as the door was about to close on a tightly packed group of people.

"Excuse us!" Frank said as he pulled open the doors. He and Callie jammed inside, drawing a carful of dirty looks.

"Four, please," Callie said pleasantly. A skinny, sour-faced man grumbled and pushed four.

The trip to the top seemed to take forever. On each floor, the elevator stopped to let off someone from the back.

Frank and Callie leaned forward as the doors finally opened on the fourth floor. But a bearded man held out his hand, preventing them from getting off the elevator.

At the same time two gunshots rang out. Behind the bearded man, a man in a dark blue suit was running as if his life depended on it.

Chasing after him, with an automatic pistol, was Edwin Squinder.

Chapter

11

"STOP HIM!" CALLIE screamed. She lunged forward.

"No, Callie! He's got a gun!" Frank yelled.

Ignoring Frank, and pushing aside the bearded man, Callie ran straight for Squinder.

Shoppers screamed and hit the floor as Squinder ran past them. His face was twisted with grim determination, his eyes focused on the man in the blue suit. He didn't even see Callie as she stuck out her foot in his path.

"Wh-o-o-oa!" Squinder let out a helpless yelp as he stumbled against Callie's foot. He tumbled onto the floor, and his gun went flying into the air. Huddled against the store windows, the shoppers gasped in horror.

"Cut!" a voice rang out. "Who's the girl?"

"I don't know, Jerry!" the bearded man by the elevator said. "She ran right past me!"

Callie looked around. Bright white lights shone

down on her from all corners of the mall. Snaking along the floor were thick electrical cords, and groups of people laughed at her from behind TV cameras. One of them screamed out, "I think we should keep it, Jerry! She's great!"

"Okay, break!" the first voice said impatiently. "Clear the area, will you? We'll shoot again in ten."

Murmuring and snickering, the shoppers got up from the floor and walked over to a tableful of snacks and soft drinks.

Callie gulped. Her face turned red as the bearded man approached her. "Okay, kid, you just broke up our scene and made me look like a fool. When are you people going to realize this is no way to get yourself on TV?"

"Sorry, sir, but I thought—I thought—"

"Never mind! Just don't let me see you here after the break, okay?"

As the bearded man stormed off, Callie turned to Frank at her side. He patted her shoulder. "Anyone could have made the same mistake, Callie. If you hadn't reacted so quickly, I would have been the one to disrupt the shooting."

At once they became aware of Squinder standing behind them. "Still you hound me!" he said, his voice edged with fury.

Frank turned around calmly and said, "It was a mistake, Mr. Squinder. You see—"

"I see plainly enough!" Squinder said between clenched teeth. "First of all, it's *Grant* around here—Tyrone Grant. But revealing my real name is part of it, I'm sure. Part of your master plan to ruin my career!"

"I wouldn't throw accusations around if I were you, Squinder," Frank said. "Not before we find out why you conspired to kill Tessa Carpenter at her party the other night!"

At that, Squinder's eyes bulged open. He clutched his chest with one hand and staggered back. "You vile, evil juvenile delinquent! How *dare* you accuse me—"

"After all, who did we find lurking around the side of the mansion with a revolver after the lights went out? Lurking near the pathway that leads to the circuit breakers in the basement, I might add!"

"Circuit breaker? What?"

"Not to mention finding your little silver-plated revolver in the woods of the Cliffside Country Club yesterday, just after Tessa was shot at!"

"Young man, you wound me to the quick! If my professional pride weren't at stake, I'd—I'd give you a sound thrashing! As for the country club, I was here all day—yes, I know it was Sunday, but they had to make up for a rainy day—waiting for a turn to play my meager role." He grabbed a sheet of paper from a nearby table. "Here, for your information, is yesterday's attendance sheet."

Frank read, "Grant, Tyrone. In: 7:30 A.M. Out: 6:35 P.M."

"I don't know why I should even dignify your other complaint, but I most certainly was *not* in the Carpenter mansion on the night of that depraved party!"

"You just happened to stop by that night, right? And despite all the people around, you thought you might get away with sneaking into the servants' cottage for your gun—"

"A loud party would be the best cover for my entry into that cottage, sir."

"Five minutes, everybody! Five minutes!" a voice called out.

Squinder looked at his watch and groaned. "I'm wasting much too much time with you two. Now will you please excuse me? You've already destroyed an otherwise marvelous day."

Without waiting for an answer, Squinder walked toward the refreshment table.

"I still don't trust him," Frank said.

"Frank, let's get out of here," Callie replied. "I don't think Squinder's about to give us any more information."

The elevator door *whooshed* open behind them, and they stepped inside. This time they were all alone.

"Okay," Frank said. "Here's the plan. I need to follow up some other leads today, but I think someone had better keep an eye on Squinder. Would you do that?"

Callie nodded eagerly.

"Keep track of everything—phone calls, meetings, any strange behavior. Follow him to his house. But make sure he doesn't recognize you.''

''How can I do that?''

The elevator opened on the parking lot. Frank went to the van and opened the sliding door. He looked both ways, then lifted up a floor panel. Underneath was a hold, jam-packed with equipment. He pushed aside a small camera, a lap-top computer, a box of diskettes containing a crime data base, a cellular mobile phone, and some magnetic metal disguise panels for the van.

''Ah, here it is,'' he said. He opened a box and pulled out a pale green uniform.

''Here's a worker's coverall. It'll be big, but if you put it on and cover your head with this''—he pulled out a beat-up baseball cap—''I think you'll be all right. You can collect papers and trash.'' He gave her a heavy-duty plastic bag.

''I've always loved high fashion,'' Callie said. She took the clothes and walked toward a nearby women's room. ''Wait here while I change.''

When Callie emerged from the women's room, the sleeves and legs of the uniform rolled up twice, Frank had to stifle a laugh. ''You'd better watch out,'' he said. ''The TV director may hire you for comic relief.''

''Just what I need, encouragement!'' Callie said. She tossed Frank her bundle of clothes and headed for the elevator.

Frank drove out of the lot, in the direction of the Bayport Museum. At the top of Cobb's Hill in the center of town, he stopped for a red light. His mind wouldn't stop racing. Now that Callie was taking care of Squinder, he began to think about Ruppenthal. There were too many loose ends—there *had* to be a way to get him to answer questions.

He was almost too involved to see a familiar car parked just beyond the top of the hill. A fiery red Lamborghini.

Frank pulled up behind it, just as someone came out of a nearby convenience store, carrying a huge stack of newspapers.

Thump. The newspapers were dropped by the side of the car, revealing Harley.

Frank gave a couple of taps on his horn and climbed out of the van. "Hi!"

Harley looked at him without expression. "I was driving by and saw Tessa's car," Frank continued. "I guess it's fixed!"

"Yes, they fixed it Saturday actually. Surprisingly it needed very little work. She wanted to go out and get it herself, but her 'bodyguard' thought she should stay in." Harley sneered at the word *bodyguard*.

"That's an awfully quick body shop!"

"The best. You get what you pay for, you know."

"What's with all these newspapers?"

"What's with all these questions? Tessa's on the front page again today, so she wanted a few copies, all right?'' Harley opened the car door and tossed the keys on the dashboard.

Frank chuckled and tried to make a joke. ''Wow, she's demanding. I guess she wants one for every room in the house, huh?''

Harley stood up and came face to face with Frank. ''Well, *you* don't seem to mind it when she demands your attention.''

''Hey, I was just kidding, Harley. Here, let me help you with the newspapers.'' Frank leaned over and began to load papers into the car.

''Get your head out of Tessa's car,'' Harley snapped. ''I don't need your help.''

''Easy, Harley, I didn't mean anything—''

''That does it! I've had enough of you.'' He gave Frank a push—a push that normally would have only rocked him back on his heels. But pressed up against the Lamborghini, he lost his balance and fell into the front seat.

Harley dove in after him, fists flying. Frank tried to swing back, but there was no room to maneuver between the dashboard and the backs of the bucket seats. He grabbed Harley's arms and thrust him backward against the steering wheel. The car horn squawked as Harley's back caught the edge of the wheel. His dark eyes blazing, Harley tried to pull Frank up and jam him against the opposite door.

But Frank yanked an arm loose and put a headlock around Harley. Trying to squirm free,

Harley jammed his knee against the emergency brake. With a click, the brake released.

As Frank and Harley fought inside, they were too busy to notice that the car was beginning to roll down the hill.

Too busy to notice it was heading straight for a gas tanker stopped at a red light below!

Chapter

12

STRUGGLING TO BREAK free, Harley fell off the front seat onto the floor. It was in that moment that Frank finally noticed the tanker.

"What the—we're moving!" Taking advantage of the distraction, Harley grabbed at Frank's collar.

"Get over it quick, buddy," Frank said as he wrenched himself free of Harley, "we're in *big* trouble."

Heooonk! Heooonk! By now the truck driver was blowing his horn, trying desperately to avoid the accident he saw coming in his rearview mirror.

The front of the Lamborghini was a tangle of arms and legs. There was no chance Frank could sit up and put on the foot brake in time. The tanker loomed larger and larger through the windshield. Frank yanked up on the emergency brake.

SCCCRRREEEEEEK! The car jerked violently, throwing Harley and Frank into the dashboard. But then it continued rolling, as if nothing had happened.

"We burned out the hand brake!" Frank said. The tanker was now fifteen feet away, still stuck at the red light. Both of its doors flew open. Screaming, the driver and his partner ran for the sidewalk.

There was only one chance. Frank reached behind him and grabbed the steering wheel. He pushed hard to the left.

The wheel moved a few inches, then clicked and stopped. The car swerved only slightly.

"It locks when there's no key in the ignition!" Harley shouted, sweat pouring from his brow. He reached down on the floor for the brake.

But it was too late for the brake. Frank felt his hair starting to stand on end as the car sped toward the tanker's left side. Then he remembered the keys on the dashboard. He grabbed them as Harley reached for the door handle. "Get off me!" he cried. "Let me jump!"

Frank jammed the key in and closed his eyes. He didn't want to see this.

A shudder pulsed through the car as he turned the key. It was still moving. Frank shoved his body against the wheel and opened his eyes. Through the right window he saw the side of the tanker *whooshing* safely by, maybe two inches away.

Harley lifted his head. Together, he and Frank

looked in the rearview mirror. The car had sailed past the intersection just as the light turned green. Peeking out from the side of a brick storefront were the tanker's driver and passenger.

With plenty of time to step on the brake now, Frank brought the car to a stop in the left lane.

"D-drive us to the side of the s-street, okay?" Harley said, unable to stop his voice from shaking.

Harley fanned himself with a newspaper as Frank pulled up to the curb. "Thanks," he said quietly.

"It's the least I could do, after the new body work," said Frank. "You may want to replace the emergency brake, though."

Harley smiled weakly. "You saved my life. How can I ever—"

"Repay me?" said Frank with a smile. "Well, you can start by being a little more friendly. We're in this together, you know."

Harley sighed. "Sorry, Frank. I guess I've been letting my jealousy show. But it seems that every time I turn around some guy is falling madly in love with my girlfriend."

"Look, Harley, I'm not in love with Tessa; I already have a girlfriend. And besides, the most important thing now is that someone is trying to kill her. If you really care that much for her, why don't you help us out?"

Harley looked stunned. "I'm *trying* to, by keeping an eye on Tessa."

"That's my brother's job. And I wouldn't worry about him. He gets that way with a lot of girls, and he's given up on Tessa by now."

"So what else do you want me to do?"

"Follow me to the Bayport Museum and help me pin down Ruppenthal. I could use some support."

Before Harley could answer, Frank hopped out of the car and ran back up the hill to his van. He passed the tanker and glanced up at the driver, who looked as if he wanted to kill him.

"Got to get those brakes fixed!" said Frank with a cheerful wave. He continued to run, without looking back.

Harley nervously fingered his hair as he followed Frank into the museum. "Look, Frank, I'm no detective, but I really think we ought to get back to the mansion. Tessa needs us. Besides, she's probably worrying about where I am."

"This won't take long," Frank answered. "We're just going to ask Ruppenthal a few more questions. Keep the heat on him."

"Personally, I don't think a wimp like Ruppenthal is very dangerous. Besides, he says he's found his agreement."

"Look, Harley, let me do the detective work. All you have to do is look menacing. Try hard."

With that he turned and walked through the museum door. Harley scowled as he followed behind.

Frank led him through the main hallway and into the outer office. The receptionist looked up from his computer. "Here to see Mr. Ruppenthal?" he asked, adjusting his glasses.

"Yes," Frank said, bluffing. "I'm Frank Hardy. I have an appointment."

The man turned back to his keyboard. "Why don't you take a seat in his office? He had an appointment, but I'm expecting him shortly."

Harley followed Frank into the empty office, where they both sat down.

"The museum looks ridiculous without that artwork, doesn't it?" Frank said.

Harley nodded absentmindedly. Beads of sweat were forming on his forehead, and he clenched and unclenched his fingers.

Finally he threw his hands in the air and stood up. "He's probably gone for the day. This is a total waste of time." He loosened his collar, looking around. "Let's go. This whole thing gives me the creeps."

Just then the silence was broken by the sounds of a door opening and footsteps in the hallway. The receptionist's voice chimed out, "First door on the left."

Harley spun around anxiously to face the door. "It's not Ruppenthal," he said.

The footsteps stopped. Two very large men in drab brown suits filled the doorway.

"We were just leaving," Harley said in a

choked voice, staring up into a broad, craggy face with a stubbly beard.

Without saying a word, the man stepped forward and grabbed Harley by the collar.

"No! No!" Harley sputtered as the man picked him up and threw him against Ruppenthal's desk. Harley let out a yell and fell onto the floor.

Instantly Frank sprang up from his chair into a karate stance. The hulking man faced him with a sinister grimace—and reached into his jacket.

"Hey, hey!" the other man called out to his partner. "What are you doing, stupid? Neither of these guys is Ruppenthal. They're way too young!"

The first man grunted and put his arm down. "Where's the big guy, punk?" he said to Frank.

"It looks as though he's left for the day."

The man lifted a clenched fist. "I'm not sure I believe you," he growled. But his partner grabbed him by the shoulder and said, "Come on, don't waste your time on this peach-fuzz! We were given bum information—let's get out of here!"

The men turned around and strode out of the doorway, leaving the scent of stale cigarette smoke in the room.

"Are you all right?" Frank asked.

Harley rose to his feet, one hand massaging his ribs. "Is this a normal day in your line of work?" he asked with a pained look on his face.

"More or less," Frank answered, his mind

already racing on to other things. "Ruppenthal's obviously in trouble with somebody—but who?"

"I couldn't even guess. Do you know what that goon was reaching for in his jacket?" Harley asked. "It wasn't—"

"A gun?" Frank smiled. "Why else would someone like that be reaching for his armpit? I don't think he was putting on deodorant."

"Look, Frank, I really don't think we should hang around here. What if they come back?"

Frank looked at this watch. "You're right. It's four-thirty anyway—Ruppenthal probably *has* gone home by now." He looked around on Ruppenthal's desk and pulled an envelope out from a stack of papers. "Here's his home address, in Short Neck. That's the next town over, just past the Carpenter mansion."

Harley shook his head violently. "I will absolutely not go with you to this man's house. I'll drive with you in that direction, but I plan to turn up Tessa's driveway—and don't try to talk me out of it!"

"Fine," said Frank with a shrug of the shoulders. "I'll follow you. Maybe my brother will change places with you for a little while."

Frank quickly copied down Ruppenthal's address, then he and Harley whisked out of the office, past a bewildered receptionist.

Within minutes the van and the Lamborghini were on their way to the Carpenter mansion.

As Frank drove up the driveway, the first thing he noticed was a black car parked at the top. He pulled up behind it and saw the MD license plate.

"Hello, boys! Where's Tessa?"

Frank turned to see Dr. Lansdale waving from the front door of the mansion.

Harley parked the Lamborghini and jumped out. "She was with Joe when I left. They were supposed to stay here."

Dr. Lansdale looked puzzled. "Well, the front door was open when I arrived, but I can't find them."

Frank and Harley gave each other a surprised look. "Why don't I check the grounds while you cover the house," Frank suggested. Harley agreed, and Frank went over to the garage.

All four doors were open. Lawn equipment and a collection of barbecue grills were scattered across half the garage. The other half was totally empty.

They must have taken the other car, Frank thought. He ran back toward the mansion, only to see Harley rushing out the front door.

"The dagger! The dagger!" he blurted out.

"What?" said Frank. "What happened to it?"

Harley's eyes were wide open in fear. "It's gone!"

Chapter

13

FRANK RUSHED PAST Harley into the parlor. The bookcase had been pushed back into place, and all the paintings hung untouched. He went straight to the sideboard. The glass case lay there, its top open, its satin cushion rumpled. But the Borgia dagger was nowhere to be seen. He turned to Harley and Dr. Lansdale, who stood dumbfounded in the doorway.

"Harley, check upstairs. Dr. Lansdale, look in the hallway and the sitting room. If we're lucky, Joe has just hidden it somewhere for safekeeping."

Frank scoured the parlor. He looked in drawers, checked under the rug, shook books down from the bookcase.

Nothing.

Soon Harley and Dr. Lansdale appeared in the doorway again. They both shook their heads.

"What do you think happened to it?" asked Harley. "You think someone kidnapped Tessa?"

"There's no ransom note, and the other car is gone. I've got to assume she and Joe went somewhere in a hurry, maybe taking the dagger with them for some reason. Any ideas where they might be?"

"The country club!" Harley said immediately.

"Or the mall," Dr. Lansdale suggested.

"Well, I guess those leads are as good as any. Dr. Lansdale, you and I will go to the club in my van. Harley, you check out the mall."

"Right!" Harley eagerly hopped into the Lamborghini. Frank helped Dr. Lansdale into the passenger seat of the van and then climbed in on the other side.

The two cars took off down the winding driveway, leaving a trail of dust. As they reached the bottom, Frank suddenly jammed on the brakes. Harley skidded to a stop behind him, barely missing the rear bumper of the van.

In front of them, trudging wearily up the road, was Joe.

"Hey, what's all the excitement about? I could use a little lift," he said.

"Joe! What are you doing here?" Frank called out from inside the van. "Where's Tessa?"

Joe shrugged his shoulders and said, "Off floating through the countryside somewhere, far away from the dark terror of Joe Hardy."

"You lost her!" Frank said.

"Well, it's more complicated than that," Joe answered. "You know, a guy tries to be on his best behavior, tries to be the ideal bodyguard, right? He keeps quiet, does his job, and then decides to make conversation—asks a dumb, innocent, friendly question—"

Frank crossed his arms. "What did you ask her, Joe?"

"Well, I was reading *Personality* magazine and I got to thinking about the actors in the movies— you know, the ones who have to do those kisses in close-up? Well, I realized these people probably don't even really know each other—"

"I don't believe this," Frank said, rolling his eyes. "Get to the point, Joe!"

Joe lowered his head. "All I did was ask how she would feel kissing a perfect stranger—"

"What?" Harley bellowed.

Joe protested, "She didn't even give me a chance to—"

"Cool it, you guys," Frank said. "Go on, Joe, what did she do after this 'innocent, friendly' question?"

"Well, she gave me a look, ran outside, and drove away. I tried to run after her. I even ran all the way into town, hoping she just stopped at an ice-cream store or something, but no luck."

"Did she take the dagger with her for any reason?"

"I don't think so. Why?"

"It's gone, Joe. The front door of the mansion was open, and the dagger was gone."

"Well, Tessa *was* storming around the house this afternoon. It's possible—"

"My guess is that someone else has it—someone who wants to use it—"

Joe finished the sentence. "On Tessa!"

Dr. Lansdale gasped. "Oh, my poor little girl!"

"Look, chances are it's nothing serious," Frank said. "She's probably at the club or driving around blowing off steam. Why don't you and Harley comb the town for her, while I take Dr. Lansdale and look for Ruppenthal. I've *got* to track him down—"

"Hold it a minute, Frank," Joe said. "You want *me* to go with Harley? Uh, I hate to say it, but that doesn't sound like the best combination."

They both glanced over at Harley pacing back and forth, his hands curled into fists. "Right," Frank said. He gave Joe the piece of paper with Ruppenthal's address. "Okay, you go with Dr. Lansdale. Try to get Ruppenthal to talk." He reached into the van. "I'll take one of the mobile phones and call you when we find Tessa."

As Frank stepped into Harley's car, Joe gunned the van down the road toward Short Neck.

"Please, Joe, I'm a little slow at this sort of thing," said Dr. Lansdale. "Why are we looking for Albert Ruppenthal?"

"Sorry, Dr. Lansdale. Frank and I can't help thinking Ruppenthal's up to something. He and Squinder are the only ones who seem to have clear motives for wanting to harm Tessa."

Dr. Lansdale stared out the window distractedly. "I still can't believe this is happening. Why would *anyone* want to murder Tessa Carpenter?"

"We're not sure. That's why we've got to follow every lead."

"And you think Mr. Ruppenthal might be behind this?"

"Possibly. The only thing that puzzles me is that he says he now has the agreement that gives the collection back to the museum."

"A bluff, perhaps?" Dr. Lansdale suggested.

"Maybe, but why?"

She shrugged her shoulders. "Well, he may know that you and Frank are guarding her. If he gets you to believe he has the agreement, then you'll think the Carpenter Collection legally belongs in the museum."

"And we'd stop guarding her if we thought she was doing something illegal."

"Precisely. This could be a means of luring you two away from her so he can attack."

Joe smiled. "You're not 'a little slow at this sort of thing' at all, Dr. Lansdale."

"Not when my Tessa's life is at stake!"

"All right, then!" Joe reached into his pocket and gave Dr. Lansdale the paper on which Frank had written Ruppenthal's address. "Let's find him."

Before long they left Cliffside Heights. Dr. Lansdale directed Joe through Short Neck and onto a road of small houses and towering maple trees. House after house looked almost identical: white shingles, freshly cut lawns, and flower gardens. But one was completely hidden by enormous green hedges.

"That's it," said Dr. Lansdale. "I must say," she added as Joe pulled up in front, "it looks sort of creepy and overgrown."

"I don't see a car in the driveway," Joe said. "We may have to wait for him."

"How do you expect to involve me in this?" Dr. Lansdale asked.

"Wait here and watch carefully while I check around. As soon as Ruppenthal lets me in, I'll sit him down and question him. I have a feeling he'll be offering me a bribe I've already refused. If he does, I'll somehow get him to offer it to me in the front room."

Joe opened the van's secret floor compartment and pulled out a small camera. "I'm setting this zoom lens for you. All you have to do is press this button and film the exchange of money. We'll build a case on Ruppenthal."

Dr. Lansdale grabbed the camera with excitement. "I'll do anything to help put this awful fellow behind bars."

"Just keep the windows up. They're tinted, so he won't be able to tell anyone's in here."

Joe walked up the empty driveway. He noticed large plastic bags of trash by the side of the house. To anyone else, it would not have seemed unusual, but Joe noticed none of the other houses had put their trash out yet.

He walked to the front door and rang the bell. No answer. He tried another time, then went over to the front windows.

One peek was all it took. Joe ran back to the van and yanked open the front door. "Quick, Dr. Lansdale, move over!"

"What is it? He's not home?"

"Not only that! There are sheets over all his furniture, and the trash is out early. He's gone all right—and it's a good bet he's on the run!"

Beeeep. Beeeep. Dr. Lansdale was startled by the sound of the mobile phone.

Joe picked it up. "Yeah, Frank . . . You did? . . . Is she okay? . . . A *what?* . . . Location? . . . We'll be right there!"

Joe threw the van into gear. The tires left a black double curve as he made a squealing U-turn.

"They've found Tessa," he said.

"What is it, Joe? Is she all right?"

Joe tightened his grip on the steering wheel. He didn't quite know how to say this. "They don't know. She's lying in a ditch by Fairground Road."

Chapter

14

Dr. Lansdale clutched the dashboard as Joe zoomed back into Cliffside Heights. The tree branches alongside the road bent in the wind as the van went by.

Fairground Road was a sharp right about a half mile past the Carpenter mansion. The van teetered sharply to the left as Joe made the turn.

The numbers on the digital speedometer changed in rapid succession. Finally Joe caught sight of two cars off to the side of the road.

"There they are!" cried Dr. Lansdale.

Joe drove onto the shoulder and stopped behind Harley's car. To their right, on the grass by the side of the road, Harley was cradling a woozy Tessa in his arms. Frank was kneeling nearby.

Dr. Lansdale threw open the van door and rushed out to Tessa, with Joe close behind.

"What happened?" Joe called out.

"We found her in the woods, almost unconscious," Frank said. "We never got to the mall."

"Why were you going on this road?" Joe said. "The mall's much closer to town."

"Harley knew about some sort of shortcut. And it's a lucky thing we came this way, or we'd never have found her."

"Is she hurt?"

"Doesn't seem so. There's practically no sign of struggle. But there is something very weird—"

Frank was interrupted by a muffled cry from Dr. Lansdale.

All eyes looked down. Dr. Lansdale was quickly brushing away hair from Tessa's forehead. Underneath was a red mark that looked like a huge, jagged scar.

Frank bent down and immediately realized it wasn't a scar at all. Shaped like a twisted lightning bolt, the mark had been drawn onto Tessa's forehead with bright lipstick.

Frank stared at it, bewildered. "It's a letter *B*," he said.

The color had drained out of Dr. Lansdale's face. "Yes," she said, nodding gravely. "It's the ancient symbol of the Borgia family."

Immediately they all fell silent.

"What are you all staring at? Tell me!" Tessa cried out. Now fully awake, she glanced from face to face with terror in her eyes.

Realizing where everyone was looking, she

shot her hand up to her forehead. With a sweep of her fingers, she wiped away some of the lipstick.

"What is this—some sort of joke? What's happening to me?"

"Everything's okay now," said Harley with a reassuring smile. "Just lie back and take it easy for a few minutes."

He rocked her in his arms, but her eyes were on Frank. "Frank, I'm scared," she said, her voice quivering. "I never should have gone off alone. But your brother—"

Frank sat down across from her. "I know. From now on, there are going to be some changes." He gave Joe a sharp, quick glance. "The three of us will stick together at all times—and Harley and Dr. Lansdale will help us. Now, tell me what you remember."

"Well, I wasn't really watching the road. All of a sudden, this big blue sedan honked its horn." Tessa choked back a sob. "I thought it was trying to pass, so I moved over. Then it pulled up alongside me and came closer and closer. I had to drive off the road."

"Did you see who was in the car?" Frank asked.

"No, I don't remember anything from that point on," she said. "I must have hit my head or something—it's all a blank."

"Nothing in the rearview mirror? Was it one or two people?"

Tessa looked confused. "Two, I think."

"Male?"

"I think so."

"Wearing business suits?"

"I don't know—maybe. Why? Do you know who it might be?"

"I have a feeling Harley and I may have run into them earlier." Frank got up and began pacing around. "But why all this Borgia hocus-pocus? We've got to put these pieces together. Tessa, we'll take you back to the house, and Dr. Lansdale can take a look at—"

"No," Tessa said sharply. "I'm too frightened to go back there. Whoever's trying to kill me can easily find me at home."

Dr. Lansdale stood up and took Frank by the arm. She led him away from the other three. "Just a minute, Frank," she said softly. "Tessa's right. Going back to the mansion isn't such a good idea, especially since the dagger has disappeared. We can't be sure the thief isn't still on the premises."

"That's true," he answered. "But don't you think Tessa's head should be looked at?"

"She seems fine, aside from being shaken up. Let's go to a diner or something for a couple of hours, where she can at least calm down. That's what she needs most."

"If you say so, Doctor. Actually, a restaurant might be a good place to sort out all the clues."

Frank turned back to Joe. "Callie's been tailing Squinder for a while. I'll go pick her up to join us. Why don't we meet you at the Argo for dinner?'' Then he smiled at Tessa. "It may not be the kind of restaurant you're used to, Tessa, but it's safe, and it'll be more comfortable than sitting here!''

Callie broke into a grin when she heard the Hardys' van pull up behind her car. She was parked a block away from Squinder's house.

Frank walked over to the car and leaned in the driver's window. "I came to relieve you from watch duty.''

"Good. I was starting to get bored. I tailed Squinder home from work, and he hasn't left since then.''

"Did you see anything suspicious?'' Frank asked.

"Not really. He reshot his scene a couple of times at the mall, then sat around watching them shoot another scene, and finally went home a couple hours ago.''

"Any visitors?''

"One guy, sort of short and greasy-looking. He had on a jacket and bow tie, wore tortoise-shell glasses. He may have been the 'Simon' whom Squinder was going to see at six o'clock.''

"Is he still inside?'' Frank asked.

"No, he left alone shortly after he arrived.''

"Good work, Callie. How about taking a dinner break?''

Callie's face lit up. "Great! I was wondering when you'd ask! Where are we going?"

"Actually," Frank called over his shoulder as he walked back to the van, "we're meeting Joe and the others at the Argo."

"Joe and the others! Just a minute, Frank, I thought *we* were going out!"

"Come on, Callie! Wait till you hear what happened!" With that, Frank started the van and rolled away from the curb.

Steaming, Callie followed him.

Frank and Callie pulled into the parking lot, just underneath broken neon letters that said TH A GO REST URANT. For a Monday night, the Argo was pretty busy. Several cars were there, and a lively clanking of plates resounded from the dining room.

In a large booth at the far corner of the dining room, Tessa, Dr. Lansdale, Harley, and Joe sat glumly reading their menus. Behind them, four teenagers were casting quick looks at Tessa and giggling.

"What took you so long?" Joe asked. "We're starving!"

Callie sat on the edge of her seat next to Tessa, and Frank sat across from them. "Looks like you're creating a little stir here," Frank remarked, referring to the table behind them.

"They must have read the paper today," Tessa said.

"It's that front-page article I was telling you about," Harley said to Frank.

"After the interview with me," Tessa continued, "that society columnist happened to stick around long enough to see the whole thing happen. And voilà—the news story of his lifetime, probably."

"And more celebrity for you," Frank said.

"As if I needed it," Tessa answered with a laugh.

As Frank and Callie opened their menus, Tessa took out a compact and freshened her makeup.

"Uh, excuse me, are you by any chance Tessa Carpenter?" They all looked up to see a middle-aged woman with a grinning man and two children.

Tessa smiled sweetly. "Why, yes. Do I know you?"

The woman and man laughed. "Oh, no! We've been reading all about you in the papers and magazines," the woman said. "My children have never met anyone famous. I just wondered—could you—I mean, would it be too much to ask you to—"

"Sign an autograph? Of course!" Tessa answered.

The woman turned to the little boy behind her. "JASON! GET MY MENU—AND ASK THE WAITER FOR A PEN! ON THE DOUBLE!" She faced Tessa again and said, "Thank you. You have no idea how much this means to him."

While they ordered and began eating their food, several other people began to drift over to the table to ask for autographs. Tessa greeted each one cheerfully.

"It's almost as if she enjoys it," Frank muttered to Joe. Callie leaned over to listen to the brothers as menus, placemats, and napkins were being signed over her head.

"Look at this," Joe answered. "They're lining up. Every single table in this restaurant!"

"Except for that nerdy-looking guy over there. He's just watching the whole thing," Frank said.

Joe and Callie turned to look at a balding man with spectacles, a bow tie, and a navy blue blazer.

Callie did a double-take and spun around, her eyes wide with excitement. "That's the guy!" she whispered.

"That's what guy?" Frank asked.

"Simon! The one who visited Squinder this evening."

Frank and Joe kept a careful eye on the man while they finished eating. Before long the autograph seekers thinned out, and soon the only people in the room were the ones at their table—and the balding man.

"Why is he just staring at our table with that weird smile?" Joe said under his breath.

"I don't know," Frank answered.

Suddenly Tessa let out a big sigh. "I don't believe this. Is *this* what my life is going to be like from now on? Smiling and signing menus? Answering policemen? You know, they're still calling and asking questions about the shooting.''

"That's one of the things I wanted to talk about,'' Frank said. "You've got to keep a distance from the press—''

"He's getting up,'' Joe said, interrupting.

Frank watched as the balding man rose from his table. He took out a wad of neatly folded and clipped dollar bills and put some on the table. Then he straightened out his blazer and made sure that a few long strands of black hair were in place over his bald spot.

Callie craned her neck around to see the man walk slowly over to their table. His eyes were focused on Tessa with a sinister glint. When they weren't looking at her, they were darting nervously from side to side.

The table fell silent as everyone realized what was happening. They all stared as the man approached.

He adjusted his collar after stopping beside their booth. Silently, he let his small eyes rove around the table, then he nodded.

With a strange half smile, he looked straight at Tessa. "Hello, Miss Carpenter,'' he said. "Edwin Squinder—or should I say, Tyrone Grant—has told me all about you.''

Frank felt every muscle in his body tense as the man reached into his breast pocket and slowly withdrew a gleaming silver object!

Chapter

15

"IT'S A GUN!" Tessa screamed. Silverware and saucers fell on the floor as Callie and Joe leapt up from the booth. Both lunged at the man with lightning-quick speed.

The man let out a frightened squawk as Callie reached him first, barreling headfirst into his stomach. He tumbled backward into a loaded tray of dirty plates, which flew across the room.

Joe immediately jumped on top of him and pinned his arms down as the man struggled desperately to protect his face. His glasses lay half on the floor, still dangling from one ear.

"Help! Help!" he cried in a high-pitched whine.

Callie bent down and pulled open his jacket to reach inside his inner pocket.

She looked down at the silver object in her hand. It was small, flat, and rectangular, with a clasp on one side.

"Are you crazy?" the man said. "It's not worth that much! Take it if you want it so badly."

Callie flipped the clasp. The top of the object sprang open. Inside, stacked neatly, was a pile of business cards. She read the top one:

SIMON LESTERMAN COMPANY
Talent Agency
Film, TV, Commercials
Phone: 555-STAR
New York   Bayport

Callie and Joe looked at each other numbly. Then Joe hopped off the man, his face quickly turning red with embarrassment. "We-we're *so* sorry, sir. *Please* forgive us. We thought you were a—a murderer."

The man sat up, his face puckered with anger and confusion. Long, thin strands of black hair hung down around his collar. "*Murderer?* Are you out of your—" As he put the silver case back in his jacket pocket, he stopped. He glanced down at his hand. Slowly he pulled the case back out. A trace of a smirk began to form on his face.

"I see—" he said slowly. "You thought my card case was a gun!" A low chuckle began to form in his throat. Nervously, Callie and Joe laughed along with him.

One by one, everyone at the table joined in laughing, as a confused busboy rushed over to clean up the damage.

"What a team, huh?" Joe said, catching his breath. "Let's check out that busboy—I think he has a bazooka!"

The busboy scrambled into the kitchen and Callie and Joe sank into their seats.

"You see, sir, Tessa Carpenter is with us," Frank explained to the man, "and there are so many—"

"Kooks after her," the man said with a toothy grin. "I understand; I've been reading the papers. Ordinarily I'd press charges, but these are special circumstances." He pulled his card case out again. "As a matter of fact, Tessa is the person I want to see."

He held out a card to her. "My name's Simon Lesterman. Talent agent. I represent Tyrone Grant. To be blunt, you're hot, Tessa. I mean that in a commercial sense. Just look at the way those people flocked after you. You've got the looks, the charm, the exotic background. You could make it big in films or TV."

Tessa looked at him with disbelief. "Is *that* why you interrupted our dinner? You just want to use my fame to make yourself a little money, don't you?"

"You wouldn't do badly yourself, sweetheart."

"*Sweetheart?*" Tessa fumed.

Lesterman shook his head with admiration and said, "Look at that. You're even gorgeous when you're mad!"

"Get him out of here!" Tessa muttered to Frank.

"All right, sir," Frank said. "We're all very tired now. Sorry for the confusion, but I think it's best Tessa's left alone now, okay?"

"Sure thing, young man," Lesterman said. Then he turned back to Tessa. "In case you want to talk, my number's on the card."

Smoothing his hair back into place, he walked out of the restaurant.

"Imagine the nerve of him," Tessa snapped. "Trying to leech onto me like that." She looked scornfully at Joe and Callie. "Thanks for saving my life from that dangerous murderer. I haven't laughed that hard since before this whole thing started."

Callie bit back the angry retort that was on the tip of her tongue. Tessa Carpenter made her furious. Tessa had been the one to shout "It's a gun!" even though Joe and she had been the ones to tackle Lesterman. And despite Tessa's big show of disgust at Lesterman's offer, Callie could see a glimmer in her eyes. The excited glimmer of someone who had just been flattered. She could easily tell that Tessa was thinking about TV fame.

Tessa put Lesterman's card in her pocketbook and looked around the room. "Check, please!" she called out to their waitress.

Frank leaned forward, finally able to ask a question that had been nagging at him. "Tessa, when you left the house today, did you know where the dagger was?"

"Of course," Tessa answered. "In the parlor."

Frank and Joe looked at each other. Dr. Lansdale and Harley exchanged a worried glance. "Uh—I think we have a new problem here," Joe added.

"What now?" Tessa said.

"The dagger is missing, and so is Ruppenthal."

Callie's eyes widened, and Tessa gasped. "This gets worse and worse!" Tessa said, burying her head in her hands. "Do you think *he* took it?"

"We're not sure," Frank said. "But don't worry, we'll find it."

"This dagger has caused me so much pain," Tessa moaned. "I'm sick of the whole situation— as soon as you get the stupid thing back, I'm going to auction it off!" She stood up from the table and walked toward the door.

Dr. Lansdale paid the bill, and they all went out to the cars.

"Please, won't you all come home with me?" Tessa pleaded. "I feel so keyed up and scared."

"I'll drive you," Harley said, putting an arm around her. He led her to the Lamborghini. "One of you can take my car."

They left the diner together—Frank in the van, Callie in her car, Harley and Tessa in the Lamborghini, and Joe and Dr. Lansdale in Harley's car.

The Lamborghini led the way—slowly, cautiously.

"All of a sudden Harley's a model driver," Frank said to himself.

Suddenly Harley's brake lights flashed. "What's he doing now?" Frank asked. "Oh, stopping for gas."

The Lamborghini slowed down and made a right turn into a gas station. The other three cars pulled over beside the curb.

Harley drove up right behind a white station wagon full of boxes and suitcases. With his back to the Lamborghini, a man was gassing up the station wagon. When he finished, he held the hose in one hand and fumbled around in his pockets with the other. Out came a set of keys and a matchbook—but no money. The man scratched his head, then opened his front door.

Honk! "Come on, move it up, will you?" Harley shouted. Annoyed, the man turned around.

"Hey, hold your hor—"

The face was instantly familiar.

Ruppenthal.

Immediately six doors slammed as everyone got out of a door.

"Stand back!" Ruppenthal screamed, a look of blind panic covering his face.

"Hello, Mr. Ruppenthal," Frank said. "You know, you're just the guy we want to see—"

"I'm warning you, don't take another step—anybody!" Ruppenthal said, holding the gas nozzle as if it were a gun. He looked at Tessa with savage eyes. "You couldn't give me a chance, could you? You couldn't at least wait until the day ended!"

Overcome with his own fury, Ruppenthal took two steps toward the Lamborghini and pressed the handle on the nozzle. A stream of clear gasoline splashed all over the car's hood. He squirted a trail of it along the ground up to his own car door.

Tessa and Harley shielded themselves and ducked away. "What are you doing, you fool?" Harley asked.

"We'll see who's the fool," Ruppenthal replied, dropping the hose onto the ground. He reached into his pocket and took out the book of matches. "All my life I've worked hard, lived by the rules. But you've changed me, Tessa Carpenter. You've turned me into a monster—a monster as ruthless as you are."

With a frantic ripping motion, he lit a match and held it poised over the gas-soaked car.

Chapter
16

"MURDERERS!" RUPPENTHAL SNARLED, as Harley and Tessa backed away. "Now toss me the keys to your cars—all of you!—or I'll blow you sky-high!"

"Has he lost his mind?" Callie whispered to Frank.

"I don't know," answered Frank. "But I don't think I want to ask him just now."

Quickly, Frank, Harley, Callie, and Joe reached into the cars, pulled out the keys, and tossed them onto the ground in front of Ruppenthal.

"Yeouch!" Ruppenthal cried as the match burned to his fingers. He threw it away from the car—and Joe sprinted toward him.

But instantly Ruppenthal lit another. "Back off," Ruppenthal said, with a maniacal grin. "It's not so easy. Thought I'd be a pushover, didn't you? Now, turn your backs."

Slowly, everyone obeyed him. Still holding the lit match, Ruppenthal climbed into his car. "Count to ten thousand, backward—and let me hear it!"

As they all started to mumble, Ruppenthal blew out the match and sped off, his tires screaming.

As soon as he heard that, Frank ran to the open door of the van. He jumped into the front seat and reached for a cigarette lighter next to the steering wheel. He pushed it in three times and then turned it twice to the right. With a jangling sound, a set of keys popped out.

He revved up the engine. "Callie, do you have extra keys?"

She shook her head no. "But my mom will bring me a set."

"Good. Drive everyone home. I'm going to get Ruppenthal."

He slammed the van into gear, made a noisy U-turn, and roared off into the street.

Looking left and right, he kept his eyes peeled for any sign of the white station wagon.

Suddenly Frank noticed something in the passenger-side mirror. A person—hanging on to the door for dear life.

He slowed down and stopped in the middle of the road. "What do you think you're doing?" he shouted.

Tessa's face popped into the window. "That was so exciting! I have *always* wanted to try that!"

"What, ride holding on to a van going sixty miles an hour?"

Tessa nodded, grinning.

"You must *like* to put your life in danger!" Frank shook his head. "Come on, get in—we're wasting time!"

She plopped into the front seat and Frank resumed the chase. He went to the end of the street, where it branched off to the center of town. He drove in the opposite direction, toward the parkway entrance. There he saw a line of cars, waiting to get on.

None of them was the white station wagon.

"We've lost him," said Frank. "He could be anywhere by now."

He spun back through the streets of Bayport, again seeing no sign of Ruppenthal. Dejected, he headed back toward the Carpenter mansion.

"That was fantastic, Frank! I felt like I was in a movie!"

"Yeah," said Frank dryly, "with one exception. Most movies have happy endings."

"Don't worry, maybe he's on his way to flee the country—and good riddance!"

"Tessa, what was he saying about 'waiting till the end of the day'?"

Tessa rolled her eyes. "Oh, how bizarre! Imagine, him calling *me* a murderer! I think this whole thing has cracked the poor man's mind!"

Soon they were climbing up the driveway to the

mansion. Frank flicked the ignition off sharply as he parked the van.

"Easy, Frank," said Tessa in a soothing voice. "I think you need to relax a bit."

"Uh—okay! Let's go inside and wait for the others!" Frank said and quickly slid out the door.

Tessa followed him into the mansion. He went straight into the sitting room and paced around.

"Well!" he said. "I have to admit, *nothing* seems to fit in this case. If Ruppenthal took the dagger, then—"

Tessa sidled up next to Frank and gently put her finger on his lips. "Shh," she whispered. "Let's forget about the case for a moment, okay?"

Frank took her hand and led her to the couch. Together they sat down. "I'm sorry, Tessa, I don't mean to hurt your feelings—but you *know* that Callie is my girlfriend. We're very happy together. This—what you're doing is not right."

"How can you say that, Frank? You're not *married* to her!"

"Tessa, don't you feel funny about all this? I mean, betraying Harley behind his back—"

Tessa looked shocked and hurt. "Harley has meant nothing to me—absolutely nothing, from the instant I met you, Frank. I can't help it!" For the first time, she moved her eyes away from Frank. "I—I love you."

Frank sank back in the couch. He watched the glistening outline of a tear form in Tessa's eye.

"I don't know what to say," he whispered.

Tessa wiped her eyes and sat up straight, a brave smile etched across her face. "Well," she said, "that's that, I guess." She fanned herself with her right hand and looked at the window.

"Imagine that," she continued. "We've been sitting here the whole time with the window shut. This room sure could use some air."

"Yes! Good idea!" Frank stood up and reached over Tessa for the front window behind the sofa. He gave a yank, but the window held fast. "Must be locked or something."

Tessa looked up from beneath him. "Oh, there's a special pin you have to pull. Here, let me help you." She reached up toward the center of the window as Frank continued to struggle.

The pin was just beyond her reach. She stood up, the back of her head practically brushing against Frank's face. There was a moment of tense stillness as Tessa tried to move the pin. Then, with a sudden movement, Tessa spun around and planted a kiss on Frank's lips.

At that exact instant the room was lit by the headlights of an oncoming car.

Frank and Tessa sprang away from each other. The sounds of slamming car doors burst the silence.

"Hey! What do you think you're doing?"

"Harley," Tessa muttered. "Perfect timing."

"Frank, is that you?"

"And Callie," Frank moaned. "We're both in luck."

The front door crashed open as Harley, Callie, and Joe entered the mansion. They had dropped the doctor off at home.

Harley's hulking form loomed in the doorway. Behind him stood Callie with a confused expression on her face. "You got what you wanted, didn't you, Tessa?" Harley shouted. "I've been in this with you all the way, risking my neck—"

"Harley, don't!" Tessa said.

"And now you think you can just toss me away like an old piece of clothing that you grew tired of!" Harley rushed forward, glaring at her with blazing eyes. "I've had enough," he growled. Then a deep laugh slowly welled up from within him.

Tessa's face blanched. She grabbed the edge of the sofa. "No—you wouldn't!"

"Really? Well, I've got news for you. You'll *never* get that dagger now!"

As Tessa froze in shock, Harley bolted outside.

"Go after him!" Tessa screamed. "He's going to spoil everything!" But Frank didn't move. He stood stock-still, head bowed, clenching and unclenching his fists. Joe stepped into the room, and he and Callie could do nothing but stare at Tessa in confusion and disbelief.

Suddenly Frank wheeled around and faced Tessa. He frowned, the face of a man furiously thinking—or just furious. "You know something about this, don't you?" he growled.

"I—what do you—me?" Tessa stammered. "How dare you accuse me—" But her protest was weak.

"Start talking, Tessa. I want to know everything," Frank demanded.

Tessa's lower lip began to quiver. She let her hair fall in front of her face as she collapsed onto the sofa. "I know who's been causing all of the murder attempts," she said in a thick voice.

"Who?" Joe burst in. "It's Squinder, isn't it?"

Tessa shook her head. "No, it's not Squinder. It's not Ruppenthal, either."

Her voice cracked as she let out a sudden sob. She raised her watery eyes toward Frank, searching for sympathy, understanding.

"Who is it, Tessa? You might as well come out with it," Frank said softly.

All at once, a rush of tears cascaded over her cheeks. She buried her head in her hands and wept. "It was Harley and me!" she blurted out. "We staged the whole thing."

She looked up to see everyone frozen in shock. The secret she'd held back could remain hidden no longer, and the words spilled out.

"Squinder was right. I did spend all the money my parents left me! How could I afford to keep up the house, let alone hired help—I *had* to fire them all. Even if I sell the mansion, it'll just be enough to pay back my loans and buy me a small house in Bayport—and then I'll have to get a job!

"That's why I took back the art collection," Tessa continued. "To sell it." Dark streaks of mascara smeared across her face as she wiped her eyes.

"Go on," Frank said. "What does this have to do with the Borgia dagger and the murder attempts?"

"The Borgia dagger was all a publicity stunt. Everything was set up by us—the shooting, the wire in the pool, the letter *B* on my forehead."

"Then why—"

"We thought if we could create a whole news event around the dagger, I'd get a fortune for it at an auction, and I'd never again worry about money. Harley has been my boyfriend since we were kids, and I promised him a cut of the auction money. But . . ." She glanced guiltily at Callie. "Then you came along, Frank. Harley could sense I was losing interest in him, that I didn't really love him, and—"

All of a sudden, she sat bolt upright and put her hand to her mouth. "Oh, no!" she gasped.

Frank, Joe, and Callie all rushed forward. "What is it?" Frank said.

"Harley—" she said, her voice catching. "Harley has the dagger. He hid it in the flower garden."

Joe looked at Frank. "Let's find him!" he said.

Immediately the brothers ran for the hallway. But before they got out of the room, they stopped in their tracks.

Silently, as if on cue, the room had been plunged into total darkness.

Chapter

17

"HARLEY! NO!" *TESSA* screamed at the top of her lungs. But she was answered by silence. "He's gone crazy, I know it!" she said. "All he wants is revenge!"

"And with that dagger, there's no telling what he'll do!" Joe added.

"Or where he is," Callie said.

Suddenly a shriek cut through the air. "Aaaaaaah!"

Frank tensed. "What's wrong?"

"Ow," Joe's voice answered. "Quiet, Tessa, it's only me! You just stomped on my foot!"

"Oh!" Tessa sighed. "I was looking for the flashlight. It's in—"

Thud. "Here." The eerie silence was broken by the sound of a drawer opening. Then a shaft of light cut through the sitting room.

"There are two flashlights here," Tessa said.

"Great! I'll take one," Joe said.

"Shh! Listen!" Callie whispered. A rhythmic *creak, creak, creak*. And then it abruptly stopped.

"Where's it coming from?" Tessa asked.

"I don't know," Joe said. "But I think we'd better deal with these lights right now, before we're dead ducks!"

Joe led them out the front and around the mansion to the cellar doors. Pulling one open, he climbed down into the room and flicked the master circuit breaker. That ought to do it, he said to himself, rushing back outside.

But the mansion just stared back at him, pitch-black.

"We're out of luck," Frank said. "He must have cut a power line."

"All right," said Joe. "If we're not going to get him to come out here, we'll just have to go in after him. Come on!"

Their flashlights blazing, all four scurried back in the front door. The hot dampness of the summer night made them feel as if everything were moving in slow motion. Musty smells of old wood and dusty carpets hung in the air as they went from room to room.

Thunk. Frank jerked his head upward at the noise above them. With a sprinter's quickness, he dashed into the hallway and up a stairway, followed close behind by Joe. At the top, he beamed the flashlight down the empty hallway.

"You're doing this all wrong, Harley," Frank

called out. "There are four of us, and one of you. It's useless. Come on out."

No response. "The noise was from the room on the right," Frank whispered. He and Joe edged down the hallway toward the room, their backs along the wall. They stopped inches from the room's doorway. It was closed. They froze for a long second.

In a burst of strength, Frank whipped around and kicked the door open. Immediately he ducked back against the wall.

The door rattled on its hinges, but no one came out. Frank held his flashlight into the room, then looked in. A four-poster bed stood neatly made, surrounded by dark wooden furniture. He stepped toward the closet and flung it open. Three lonely winter coats rocked back and forth with the updraft from the door's movement.

"Disappeared," Joe said.

Frank looked out into the hallway. "Where are Callie and Tessa?" he asked.

As if in answer, a piercing scream rang out from the other end of the floor.

Frank and Joe charged down the hallway in the direction of the noise. Out of one of the rooms came gasps of shock. They rushed inside, and Frank shone the light on a figure crumpled on the floor.

"Callie! Are you all right?" Frank asked, kneeling next to her.

"I—I think so," she answered, her left hand covering her ear.

"Let's see." Frank took her hand away and looked at her ear. "It's bleeding a bit, but doesn't look too bad."

"What are you doing here alone?" Joe asked.

"After you guys ran off, Tessa and I thought we'd take the back stairway. She went straight up to the third floor, but when I got to the second, I thought I heard a noise."

"So you came into this room, without a flashlight?" Frank said.

Callie nodded. "Anyway, the minute I walked in here, I heard someone call Tessa's name in a low voice behind me. I turned around and saw Harley's outline—then he nicked me with the dagger. When I screamed, I think he realized who I was, and he tried to pull back. Then he ran out of the room, cursing." She shuddered. "I think he's gone completely crazy."

"You're lucky he didn't get more than the ear," said Joe.

"We can't just stand here," Callie pleaded. "He's vicious! If I had been Tessa he would have killed me."

"We've got to get to Tessa!" Joe said. "She's alone!"

Suddenly from upstairs came another scream. Even as it echoed through the house, Frank, Joe, and Callie were flying up the back stairs. They ran into a large attic room.

There, beneath the sloping wood-beam ceiling, Tessa and Harley stood at opposite ends of an oak table.

"Get away from me, you beast!" Tessa shrieked. Harley stood poised with the Borgia dagger, faking from side to side, looking for a way to run around the table.

"Drop it, Harley!" Frank called out. Harley looked toward the door, into the glow of Frank's flashlight.

"Yeeeeaaaaaggghh!" Screaming, Harley hurled himself across the table. He caught Frank at stomach level and tackled him to the ground. The light zigzagged crazily around the room as the flashlight clattered to the floor. Frank grabbed for it, but it rolled out of his reach.

"How about a little taste of the Borgia curse?" Harley hissed as he raised the jeweled dagger.

Joe grabbed the flashlight off the floor and pointed it directly at Harley and Frank—in time to see Frank push Harley's arm back. The dagger flew against the corner wall.

All motion in the room followed it. Frank, Harley, Joe, Callie, and Tessa dove into the corner. A tangle of arms and fingers reached out toward the dagger, but only one person's hand closed around it.

"Get back! He's got it!" Frank yelled. He, Joe, and Callie fell away as Harley brandished the dagger over his head.

Then, with a sudden lunge, he pushed Tessa to

the ground. The dishes stored in the old break-front behind him rattled as he pulled her in front of him. She let out helpless sputtering sounds as Harley locked his elbow around her neck.

"You're—ch-cho—king—me!" she was able to say.

Frank and Joe rushed toward her.

"Stand back!" Harley barked, holding the dagger to Tessa's throat. The brothers stopped in their tracks.

"It had to come to this, Tessa, didn't it?" Harley said, his voice rising to a high-pitched frenzy. "We had it planned so perfectly. We both could have been so happy for the rest of our lives. But you destroyed it—you destroyed it with your greed. Admit it!"

"H-Harley, stop it!" Tessa said, struggling to breathe. "You're out of your mind!"

Harley tightened his grip. "Admit how you betrayed me. Admit that you were going to take all the auction money for yourself and leave me with nothing—that you pretended to fall in love with Frank Hardy as an excuse to break up with me!"

"No! Please!" Tessa cried.

With a choked cry, Harley pushed her violently against the cabinet.

Whock! The doors flew open. Harley shot a glance upward, just in time to see the shower of plates and silverware flying toward his head.

Tessa wrenched herself loose and hit the

ground. The sound of crashing metal and porcelain was like an explosion.

Joe turned off the flashlight, and pandemonium broke loose.

It was only a matter of seconds that the fight lasted, but it ended with a dull thud.

When Joe shone the flashlight again, he was standing over Harley, who lay rock-still on the floor, the dagger dangling from his right hand.

"Oops. I, uh, I guess his head got in the way of the flashlight," Joe said with a guilty grin. "Hope he's okay, though."

"He'll be all right," Frank said, pulling Tessa away.

"He almost killed me!" she cried between gasps.

"Well, he's not too dangerous now," Frank reassured her. "At least until he wakes up."

From outside came the sound of a car door closing.

"Who could *that* be?" Callie asked.

"If we're lucky, it's the police, checking out some clue," replied Joe.

Tessa fell against Frank, shaking and trying to swallow breaths. He put his arm around her, and with Joe's help, they sat her down away from the mess.

"Please forgive me, Frank," Tessa said. "Harley was wrong. I did everything out of love for you—a love that was foolish and selfish—"

"Just a minute!" Callie broke in, pointing her

flashlight at all three of them. "There's something missing here. Maybe Harley did fire the shot at the country club, and put the wire in the pool, knowing the socket didn't work. But it couldn't have been only Harley who pulled that stunt at the party. How could he have shut off the electricity *and* pushed the statue down?"

Frank and Joe looked at Tessa. The sound of footsteps on the back stairs were like muffled drumbeats.

"And," Callie went on, "how could Harley have hidden the dagger? Frank was with him the whole time when he found it was missing!"

Instead of answering, Tessa gazed tensely at the door. A dull light illuminated the hallway as the footsteps approached the room and stopped.

"Don't bother to get up. I'll only be a minute," a voice said.

Frank, Joe, and Callie swung their heads around as the room was lit in a soft, flickering glow. Holding a kerosene lantern in her left hand, Dr. Lansdale smiled evilly. In her right hand was a gun.

"Here, my friends," she said with a cold glint in her eye, "is your missing link."

Chapter

18

DR. LANSDALE SNICKERED. "Just think, for a few brief moments you'll have been the only other people on this earth who knew about my almost-perfect plan."

"You!" Callie said under her breath.

"What's the matter? Didn't think a doddering old lady doctor had any guts?" She shook her head and gave Tessa a disgusted look. "You really blew it, Tessa. Everything had been going like clockwork. I was hoping this wouldn't have to get messy."

"You wouldn't kill us," Joe said.

"Oh? The three of you—stand together near Harley," Dr. Lansdale ordered. "Tessa, you move away. This will look like Harley shot them and then put a gun to his own head." She chuckled. "I can see the *Times* now—'HEIRESS'S JILTED BOYFRIEND IN TRAGIC BLOODBATH OVER LOVE.'

It'll be just another saga in the long history of the Borgia curse.''

Slowly Frank, Joe, and Callie stood up and walked toward Harley.

"Please, Aunt Harriet, I never expected—"

"That's enough, Tessa! Now get over here. Stand right by me!"

As Dr. Lansdale pointed her gun at Frank, Tessa meekly got up. "I—I tried to protect you, Aunt Harriet. I was all set to take the rap and leave you out of it. No one would have gotten in any real trouble—"

"And you'd kiss my money goodbye as Ruppenthal took everything back, right?" Dr. Lansdale shook her head. "Sorry, my naïve little girl."

Frank and Joe surveyed the room with their eyes, looking for some distraction, some way of escape. . . .

"Hands high and eyes straight at me!" Dr. Lansdale said sharply. "I wasn't born yesterday, you know."

The three of them had no choice. Dr. Lansdale's lantern cast ghostly shadows on their faces as they silently obeyed. Slowly, they edged toward the motionless Harley, as Tessa shuffled closer to the door.

"Faster! What is this? Am I in a nursing home?" Dr. Lansdale said impatiently.

Tessa hung her head as she obediently approached Dr. Lansdale.

"I hope you're competent enough to hold this," Dr. Lansdale said. She handed Tessa the lantern and then placed both hands on the gun. With a strong, steady motion, she raised it—and aimed it between Frank's eyes.

"What a waste," she said with a sigh. "This is the smart one." Carefully, she cocked the gun.

From the deepest reaches of her soul, Callie unleashed a long, terrified wail. She pressed her eyes tightly shut.

It was hard to tell what happened next. The room got brighter. A shot rang out. There was a scream.

Callie opened her eyes. "Frank!" she yelled. She turned to look at her boyfriend. His body was still standing. His arms were still raised in the air. His mouth hung open in amazement.

Callie looked over to the door. Tessa had raised the flame in the lantern to full blast—and was holding it in front of Dr. Lansdale's face.

"Enough! Enough!" Tessa shrieked, pushing the lantern into Dr. Lansdale's face again and again. "This was your idea in the first place! You turned Harley into an animal, you ruined my life—and now I see you for what you really are—"

"You spoiled little twit!" With a slow but well-placed swing of her left arm, Dr. Lansdale ripped the lantern out of Tessa's hand. It flew through the air and smashed underneath the oak table.

"I really didn't want to have to do this," Dr. Lansdale snarled.

She swung the gun at Tessa.

Now there was no question—it was the right time. Callie leapt across the room. With a swift chop, she attacked Dr. Lansdale's arm. The gun crashed to the floor and slid across the room.

Howling desperately, Dr. Lansdale dove after it. She reached for it, only to find a foot had gotten there first. Callie's foot. She kicked the gun sharply toward the lantern.

All eyes followed the gun—and suddenly the room became dead still. The gun was circled by flames. Flames that the lantern had thrown onto the dry, old floor and table.

"Put it out! Somebody!" Tessa yelled.

"Where's the fire extinguisher?" Joe asked urgently.

"Fire extinguisher? I don't—"

That was all Frank and Joe needed to hear. "Come on! This place is going to catch like a pile of dried twigs!" Frank shouted. He grabbed Callie and ran out, pulling Dr. Lansdale. Joe lifted Harley and carried him into the hallway.

They shot down the stairs and barged out the front door.

On the lawn was a squad car. Two policemen emerged from it and sprinted toward the mansion.

"Here they come!" a voice called out in the muggy night air. "Two white males, age eighteen to twenty-one—hold it, it's Frank and Joe Hardy!"

Cursing and scratching, Dr. Lansdale struggled to wrench herself from Frank's grip. "Let go of me, you disrespectful young—"

Frank ignored her as they stumbled toward the squad car. "Officer Riley—the third floor is on fire!" he shouted.

"I've got eyes, Frank," Riley replied. "I've just called the fire department." He lowered his brows in a scowl. "I happen to have ears too. We heard a shot. Who's going to be the one to explain it?"

"Officer, look what this young hoodlum is doing to me—" Dr. Lansdale yelled.

"Hey, hey, now!" Officer Riley said. "Have you gotten carried away, Frank? Let her go, she's safe now!"

"Officer Riley," Frank said, "this woman fired the shot you heard. It was meant for me."

Riley looked from Frank to Joe with suspicion. "*This* woman?"

"Wait a second!" Joe interrupted. "Why did you come here?"

Officer Riley held up a silver-plated revolver in a clear plastic case. "Exhibit A, from the Cliffside Country Club shooting. Our ballistics experts traced this to the Carpenters. Officer Novack and I were coming here to ask Miss Carpenter a few questions."

"Yes, it's hers!" Dr. Lansdale cried out. "Arrest her! It's the Borgia curse—it's still following her! Arrest them all!''

"Ah, it's all clear now," Riley said, sarcastically. "We've got an ancient curse, an elderly lady who shoots young men, and a girl who's shot at by a person using her own gun."

"And therein lies—" Joe began.

Riley rolled his eyes. "A long story, I know." He grabbed Tessa and Dr. Lansdale. "Come on, you're both coming to the station house. It's going to be a long night."

But Tessa's eyes were fixed in sheer horror at the smoke that was now billowing from the third floor. "I—can't—leave," she said, in almost a whisper.

"It's her house," Officer Novack said. "Let's at least wait till the fire department gets here."

"Fire department!" Dr. Lansdale cackled. "If they're anywhere near as bright as you fellas, we'll be here all night!"

Officer Novack gave Dr. Lansdale a long, hard glance. "You've got some explaining to do," she said.

Dr. Lansdale folded her arms as Officer Riley reached for his handcuffs. Orange flames began to dance from the rooftop of the mansion. From the bottom of the hill came the sound of sirens.

Behind Frank was a soft, sniffling sound. Frank turned to see Callie, sobbing.

"I-I'm just a little shook up," she said.

"With good reason," Frank said. He wrapped

150

his right arm around her and looked deep into her moist eyes. "*You're* the reason we're all alive."

Callie wiped away a tear and smiled. "Well, the Hardy family aren't the *only* good crime-fighters in Bayport!"

Together they watched the burning mansion with a bittersweet sadness.

Joe buttoned his leather jacket and rolled up the window of the van. "What kind do you want to get?" he asked.

"Now let's get this straight," Frank answered sharply. "This Halloween candy is only for kids who come to the house, okay? I don't want this to be like last year, when you finished it all off yourself!"

"Fine, fine," Joe said as Frank steered the van out of the brisk October air and into the shopping mall.

They were alone in the elevator as they took it up through the mall. Slowly it came to a stop at the third floor.

"Watch it, Joe!" Frank shouted. They both peeled to opposite walls as the door slid open to reveal a short, bald man with a machine gun.

"Trick or treat!" a voice squeaked from behind the mask.

"Honey, come on," a woman behind him said, urging him into the elevator. "These boys are shopping. Wait till we get home."

Frank and Joe chuckled as they walked through

the floor. "Looked a little like Albert Ruppenthal," Frank said.

"Yeah, except Ruppenthal's smiling a lot more since he got that court injunction to get the Carpenter collection back."

"Well, he'll be spending a lot more time in court, what with that suit against Tessa for destroying the Greek statue—"

"And the suit against Harley for hiring those two thugs to rough him up!"

Frank smiled. "What a day that was. You should have seen the look on Harley's face when he knew they were coming, and we were the only ones in Ruppenthal's office!"

"And little did you know Ruppenthal saw the whole thing through the window, walking back to the museum from lunch that day."

"Yeah, no wonder he wanted to get out of town so fast."

Motorized witch models flew around a replica of a haunted mansion in a toy store window they passed.

Joe looked at it briefly and turned to Frank. "I hear they've repaired the damage to the third floor of the Carpenter place. Has Tessa finally decided to get an apartment and turn the old house into a museum?"

"Those were the rumors a while back," Frank said with a shrug of his shoulders. "The last time I spoke to her was at Harley and Dr. Lansdale's sentencings. She said she had let the fire insurance policy lapse on the mansion, so the repairs had to come from her own pocket. Now she's more broke than ever. She's just lucky most of the artwork survived."

They stopped to watch a soap opera flickering from seven TV sets in a store window. A young blond man in a tuxedo was trying to comfort a woman in a mink coat. The woman was sobbing hysterically, her head buried in a sofa pillow.

"I wonder what ever happened to Tessa," Joe mused.

"Got some sort of job, I guess," Frank suggested.

"But what? What kind of job could someone like that possibly be qualified to do?"

They watched the soap opera quietly for a few more minutes. The blond guy stormed out, revealing a butler who was eavesdropping.

The brothers began to turn away. But suddenly their attention was drawn to the TV again. In a shrieking rage, the rich young woman burst up from the sofa and faced the butler.

Both Frank's and Joe's eyes popped open as they found themselves staring into seven images of Tessa Carpenter's face.

"I guess that answers my question," Joe said. "Looks like she must have turned to Simon Lesterman to help her."

Tessa stormed around the room, sometimes screaming and breaking furniture, sometimes pleading. The butler pleaded with her to stop.

"It's just like she is in real life," Frank said.

"And don't look now, but the butler is played by Edwin Squinder!"

As Joe watched Tessa and Squinder's furious overacting, his mouth slowly formed the trace of a smile. "You know," he said, "I think they're both finally where they belong."

The sound of Frank and Joe's laughter echoed through the mall, mixed with the muffled screaming from the TV set, as they raced each other to the candy store.

Frank and Joe's next case:

When the Hardys win an all-expenses-paid trip to sunny Spain, they look forward to playing on the beaches. But when their tour guide disappears and foreign agents start closing in on them, playing is more work than it seems.

Frank and Joe investigate their "good luck" in winning the contest—and in meeting Elena, a beautiful Spanish girl. The more they dig, the more it looks as if they've been set up in a dangerous game of espionage. Still worse, both sides now consider them security risks—and in the spy business, security risks don't live to a ripe old age!

Can Frank, Joe, and Elena clear themselves? Or will rival spymasters clear them off the board? Find out the answer in *Too Many Traitors*, Case #14 in The Hardy Boys Casefiles.

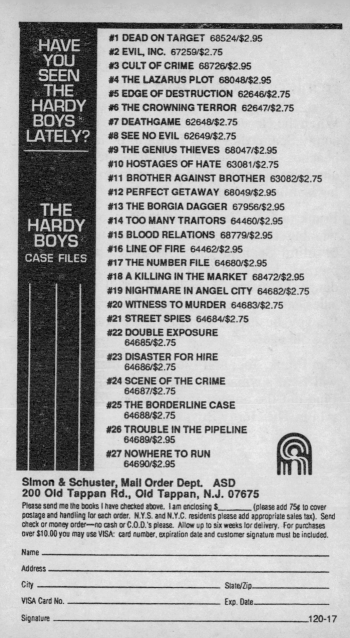